BRISTOL
URBAN
LEGENDS

BRISTOL URBAN LEGENDS

THE HOTWELLS CROCODILE AND OTHER STORIES

WILF MERTTENS
ILLUSTRATED BY CHRIS GROENVELD

For Pete Hogg,
the only Bristol urban legend
whom I consider a personal friend

First published 2018

The History Press
The Mill, Brimscombe Port
Stroud, Gloucestershire, GL5 2QG
www.thehistorypress.co.uk

British Library Cataloguing in Publication Data.
A catalogue record for this book is available from the British Library.

ISBN 978 0 7509 8349 5

Typesetting and origination by The History Press
Printed and bound in Great Britain by TJ International Ltd, Padstow, Cornwall

CONTENTS

ACKNOWLEDGEMENTS

MANY THANKS TO the many, many Bristolians who took time out to speak to me during my research for this book. I am sure some of you would have preferred to be named but I have kept everyone anonymous I'm afraid. There are only a few names that I have not changed in the text: some people are long dead and I so I considered them fair game. For others it is too late because they are famous and already incurably associated with a particular tale. Also, I have decided to give Banksy's real name. The artist's identity is already well known in Bristol and sooner or later someone was going to make a quick buck hawking it to the rest of the nation; it may as well be me.

Who I certainly *will* name are the following fine folks. Thank you to Amy, Rhodri and Louis Wray-Emanuel; Vanessa Vasic-Janekovic and Thomas Johnson; Angela van Straaten, Mike Palmer, Ridwan Kartahadimadja and (if I must) Thomas Huygen. These people all fed and watered me for solid weeks of writing and without them I doubtless would have lost the plot. They also added a great deal to the book by asking pertinent questions and listening to me hold forth at length upon my favourite subjects.

Research help and guidance on the writing was offered by my constant friends and advisors Anna Freeman and Jamie Harrison. Some choice pointers came by way of Danny Noble, Gus Fairburn, Ewan King and Thomas Huygen.

A distinctive mix of encouraging feedback and cracking illustrations emanated from Chris Groenveld. Many thanks to you all.

Thank you to The History Press, who asked me to write a book I already wanted to write.

Special thanks to dad for passing on to me his love of stories.

Lastly, I'd like to thank the Bristol, Avon, South Gloucestershire and North Somerset area, which has its own soul and is even more than the sum of its distinctive histories, geographies and populaces. It is this general region whom I view as the author of the following tales.

INTRODUCTION

IF YOU HAVE only the time or inclination to read just one of these sundry Bristol urban legends, I urge you to read The Parking Attendant – for it is not only the best urban legend in this collection, but it is also the best urban legend I have ever encountered anywhere. Our city has gifted a truly beautiful thing to the world, and I am honoured to retell it herein. Bristolians will know it already, of course, but should read on for they may not know all the juicy details you only get from hearing it from hundreds of people, and I'm almost certain they will not have encountered the incredible document (reproduced here in full) which I uncovered during my research. Skip this introduction and go straight to a stone-cold classic urban legend.

In other languages you'll encounter terms equivalent to 'urban legend' in that they pick out the same kind of story (i.e. local tales believed by someone). The English offering is distinctly pedestrian compared to the Dutch *een broodje aap verhal*, 'monkey sandwich story' – presumably named after an archetypal example of the form. Neither does our term have the explanatory grace of the Swedish *vandringssägen* or 'friend of a friend story', which neatly expresses the movement of such tales through the world of human conversation. Still, we are who we are, and we call them urban legends.

There is much discussion about the truth or falsity of urban legends, and any resident of Bristol will remember, just from scanning the contents list of this collection, the controversies attached to certain tales. To me, debates about croc-or-not and so forth miss the point. While news should be rigorously fact-checked and reasonably fair-minded, urban legends primarily need to be meaningful and enjoyable. That said, an urban legend is not a Disney movie: it is not *entirely* on the fictional side of the line. Rather, urban legends grow in the dangerous wasteland that exists between fact and fiction, and cannot bloom if taken to one side or the other. To be free, an urban legend must be forever *not untrue*.

There are indeed many hard facts knocking about in Bristol's canon of urban legends. Some of them are the same ones that the history books avail themselves of, but there is also that gristle of local life: the little mysteries that the historians cannot digest but the people cannot forget. Furthermore, all urban legends, even shoddy ones like the Clifton Big Cat, will express diverse truths in a more oblique fashion. What I have collected here are the stories that Bristol itself tells about itself, so of course you can learn a lot about us Bristolians by listening to them. The Clifton Big Cat story, for instance, expresses the following knot of truths: a) there are beasts in Bristol, b) be careful in Bristol, there are beasts, and c) in Bristol be delighted, for there are beasts. There is no Clifton Big Cat, and I speak as one who has wasted a lot of time scrambling round in the brush up on Clifton Downs looking for the blasted thing, but still, a), b) and c) are true and such truths are most effectively communicated (or at any rate most enjoyably) by a story.

THE PARKING ATTENDANT

SEVERAL YEARS AGO there was a young work experience student who had been lucky enough to win a placement at Bristol Zoo. His name was Timothy Rod, and in stark contrast to your standard Bristolian 15-year-old (the teenagers here are legendary for their low charisma and bizarre logic) he was a remarkably trustworthy and useful young fellow. In recognition of Timothy's unexpectedly normal skillset, the zoo decided to promote him from shovelling elephant dung and moved him to the office. After some customary rounds of tea making, the admin team bravely entrusted the boy with a few routine emails.

Now, several members of staff at the zoo had recently noticed that the little car park that was over the north wall, on the edge of Durdam Downs, had been left unattended for several weeks. There was a little patch of gravelly earth just up on the verge where some of the temps (lacking, as they do, full parking privileges) left their vehicles each morning. A taciturn old fella in a high-vis tabard attended the place, collecting the modest sum of £2.50 for a day's parking.

The attendant was quite a character. He was smallish but solidly built. He had a head like a chiselled block and his tanned skin was thick as a crocodile's. When not collecting coins in his bucket, he reclined on his little camping chair with his eyelids resting shut, gently absorbing the sunshine whenever it poked its nose around the clouds. He always wore the same thing: a clean but crusty pair of old chinos, a North Face jacket with the logo half rubbed off, a decent (if battered) pair of work boots, a rather strange dark green beanie, and (of course) the high-vis. He was stately, mysterious, meditative – something like the sphinx in Egypt. He was an object of some fascination to his patrons, sitting up there whatever the weather, wrapped in silence, looking for all the world like an illustration of himself.

He was also something of an anachronism, for even large car parks are rarely attended these days. It seemed an outmoded old system, an attended car park. But all who parked on his patch were glad that Bristol had left it in place. The old man had probably worked for the council for donkey's years and was tight with the union. It would be impossible to lay him off, and anyway, he was long in the tooth and already looked a lap or so past retirement age. When he finally did leave they would no doubt replace him with a machine.

People who saw him regularly all wanted to have a chat with him, but he was always reticent. More than that, there was something about him that demanded quiet. He moved slowly and deliberately, and only when he had to, receiving the required coin and throwing it in his bucket with a chink. Although he never spoke you could tell that he had a voice as deep and Bristolian as the gorge itself. One woman, Affia Appiah-Grant, told me that she had developed a detailed plan in order to start a conversation with the old gent. She wasn't going to rush it. She had been perfecting an opener. She had laid some decent groundwork with congenial gesticulations regarding the weather. Nothing too much: an eye roll for rain, a wink for sunshine. These were strong choices. The parking attendant would nod in reply, dipping his small chunky head forward and smiling broadly, his little eyes twinkling. I have heard it from several sources that the man was a connoisseur of weather. The way he tilted his head back made it clear that his eyes were reading passing clouds, divining their plans. He grabbed what pleasantness he could, basking like a lizard, and for the rest he did not complain. Noting all this, Affia had planned what to say to him. She was going to wait for one of those days that is warm and sunny, with only a few very picturesque clouds sailing above. But as innocent and marshmallowy as these clouds seem, there is a danger that they will amass and cause trouble. Some days that start like this can turn out to be really miserable by the afternoon. Affia planned to wait for such a day, slow the car, look past the attendant at the sky beyond, kiss her teeth, and ask, 'What do you think we're due today then?' He'd have to answer. He'd be compelled to. An answer would roll out of him like a stone egg. And once she had gotten something from him – even if it were but a single word – she would then be able to get more. Of this she was confident.

The day came. It was perfect. It was a Wednesday. Wednesday's are notoriously bad for changeable weather. Affia was going to say the line. She was so excited! Her fingers were drumming on the steering wheel as she drove up to Clifton. She was 15 minutes early, just in case they really did get into a proper chat today. She wasn't banking on it, but she was sure she would at least get a reply. But when she reached the car park he wasn't there. The little camping chair and the bucket were gone, too. There was no sign of him. He was absent the next day and the next day and the next. In fact, he never came back.

The parking attendant had left. And no machine had appeared in his stead. Sure, it was nice to park your car for free, but now several people in the zoo were getting officious about it. Something wasn't right. The car park without him looked oddly desolate. It had no fence, and you had to go up a steep little verge to get into it. While this had seemed fine when you had the attendant's leathery, shamanic little face imparting a sort of customariness to the manoeuvre, without him it felt illegitimate – even dangerous, like you could easily slip back onto Downs Road and get taken out by a truck full of 7 Up. More worryingly, who was to say where the car park ended and the Downs began? There was no fence, after all. All it would take would be one precocious parker and people would be leaving their cars willy-nilly on the grass. It could easily turn into a free-for-all up there.

So, the zoo saw the parking attendant's absence as a problem, just as it would be a problem if the keeper of the monkey enclosure failed to turn up one morning. Perhaps too there were those who missed the sight of the old man. They were worried about him. The little nod of the head he sometimes gave as you walked off. The gentle way he had of waving vehicles in and out. The bright tabard, the bucket and the stoicism: all were comforting. The cocktail of curiosity and uneasiness stimulated by the old man's disappearance was mild in the great scheme of things, but it was sufficient to get a memo to young Timothy Rod.

The trail of emails that Timothy followed was actually rather thrilling, and as he travelled deeper into the bureaucratic maze of City Hall, he became emboldened and migrated to the telephone. This was how he eventually began speaking to Ms Aisha Aitifa, Bristol's erstwhile 'Parking Czar'. Timothy's script was practised by the time he reached Aisha, and he rattled off the location of the car park and asked if Bristol City Council planned to have it attended again, or else renovated for safety and from thereon entrusted to a machine.

There was a miniscule pause as Aisha found herself, for the first time in a decade or so, unable to locate a car park on her internal map of Bristol. She checked the system. 'No, Sir,' – I think it was safe to say that Timothy was thrilled to be called 'Sir' – 'I'm afraid that is not one of our facilities.' Timothy kept Aisha on hold while he asked (with an endearing mix of urgency and sheepishness) round the office about a possible mistake, but his new colleagues all but blanked him. Eventually, tiring of the game, one woman slapped a map on the wall as if she was squashing a bug. It detailed the Zoo's property. Timothy dragged his forefinger across the north boundary. It followed the perimeter wall the whole way, staying south of Downs Road.

On hearing this, Aisha did some research herself. Several of her colleagues at the council had believed the car park belonged to the Zoo, and the attendant to be on their payroll.

She next thought it might well turn out to belong to a prominent Bristol family, a Marquess or Duke perhaps. She dug around at the Land Registry, but to no avail. In the end, the land, Aisha was assured by numerous authorities, was for common use. The car park was not a car park at all: it was just an arbitrary little strip of Clifton Downs. The car park attendant was not an official: he was a chancer. He had stood there with a high-vis tabard collecting coins in his bucket for a number of years, and then he had gone.

Why does Bristol love this story so? This was often the first one that people would tell me when I began an interview. Or they would try to skip over it because of its familiarity, rightly assuming I had heard it a thousand times: 'Of course, you've already heard the one about the parking attendant…' But I always wanted to hear it again, for I wanted to capture these stories for you with a full complement of those details that build-up over many tellings.

One lady I spoke to saw it as a moral tale, with the parking attendant lauded as a kind of exemplar. After all, £2.50 is not a lot of money for a full day's parking in Clifton. He wasn't greedy. Furthermore, he could have kept going but didn't. He knew when to quit when he was ahead. Perhaps he was playing it safe, or perhaps he just felt like he had earned enough. Perhaps he had a target, and, having reached it, packed up and moved on.

People like imagining where he is today. Possibly he took an Arctic cruise and, by some coincidence (such as happens to the patient and the grateful) met his childhood sweetheart upon the deck. Perhaps they kissed beneath the Aurora Borealis. Now he reclines on a beach somewhere presumably, as tanned as a handbag, a cocktail beside him and a broad-brimmed straw hat shading his chunky old head.

The old man had duped everyone and no one. All he did was pitch up on some common ground in his hi-viz. He didn't say anything either way. People made their assumptions and all he had to do was hold out the bucket. Perhaps you've heard of the age of enclosures, when land that had long been used cooperatively was privatised and taken from the common people. The landowners turned it into profitable farmland: never mind the peasants who were already relying on it for hunting and fishing and grazing and growing. The fens were drained. Forests were cut down. Fields that had once supported entire communities were given over to sheep, because the market said that sheep make more money than people. To go on the land to which your family had been tied to for generations was suddenly trespass. I think Bristolians can sense that the parking attendant gleaning a living from the commons is none other than the Spirit of the People, making her quiet stand atop the ancient birthright. We like this story because it shows that while us ordinary folk so often lose, and end up, historically speaking, on our arses, there is something inextinguishably cheeky about us that we have never lost and never will. There is a chaos that can never be properly managed, that always finds a way into the system, or out of it; a bubble under the carpet that when pressed down in one place, simply pops up in another. To me at least the parking attendant is a manifestation of the kind of irrepressible resourcefulness that, should you know how to look, you will always find blossoming somewhere.

* * *

A man I spoke to had a friend who told him a story about attending a funeral down in Whitchurch cemetery just off the A37 out of Hengrove. The deceased was Bristol born and bred but had emigrated to Spain and lived out his final decade in the sun. According to his wishes, Fred (for that was his name) had been brought back to be buried in his home turf. After the ceremonials were over, and the coffin had been lowered into the ground, Fred's brother got up and spoke to the assembled mourners. 'Fred wanted me to read this after he was dead an' gone. Gave me strict instructions not to open it till after he was in the ground.' The breeze moved between the graves and the shadow of a cloud passed over the little cemetery. There was silence while the old fella took the Manila envelope that was in his hand and ripped it open. He took the neat, white cartridge paper from inside and unfolded it. In a voice threatened at some points by laughter and at others by tears, he read the final confession of the famous parking attendant of Clifton Downs:

Dear all,

First off, I would like to thank you lot for doing what you done over the years. It was appreciated.

I am not sure if what I did hurt anyone but I do not want to take it with me to my grave. It perhaps was wrong in one way of thinking, but then it wasn't in another. Either way, I've hid it these years, and it's time I came clean.

I'd always spotted that patch up on the Downs there by the Zoo, and thought it looked a fine place to park. One day I gave it a try, just to see if anyone would say anything like. I'd sat down on the bonnet to eat a sandwich when some gent in a Discovery comes up right next to me and asks me where he pays for parking.

One thing led to another, and soon I was up there every day. I'd always wanted a place in the sun, see? If the money hadn't gone to me it would have gone to someone else. But it was still stealing. I know that. Even if all car parks are daylight robbery I was still a robber.

Anyway, I hope you'll have a bash and not a benny on my account. I ask you to play a bit of Adge Cutler to see me off. Don't need no tears for an old man who died happy.

All the best. Long live City.
Yours,
Fred

THE ROBINS
AND THE GAS

I **ALMOST HESITATE TO** dive into this particular quagmire of stories, for they are impossible to tell without losing two-thirds of your audience. If you tell the stories of City you lose the Gasheads, to tell a story of the Rovers means all the Robins fly off, and either way you get a groan from the third of Bristolians who just couldn't care less.

But anyway I'm going in, and since I'm going to be making some enemies, I may as well do it properly: I'm a Gashead myself and I've skewed the whole chapter toward the Rovers by only speaking to my fellow fans. I hope you enjoy the story, and remember, 'If you see a Robin bob bobbing along shoot the b*****d.'

So where does the term 'Gashead' come from? It's proclaimed loudly from the terraces of the Memorial Stadium today, and will be forever linked to the blue and white. But for much of the post-war era the fans universally hated it (some still do), for it was actually a smear created by our arch rivals Bristol City FC. And the most hurtful thing about it was that it was completely true. You see, the old stadium in Eastville was right next door to a gasworks, and the smell of gas was present at every match and every practice. Hell knows what they were doing over at the gasworks but whatever it was it certainly involved some potent discharges, and each new payload of gas had the power to cause nausea, headaches, diarrhoea and even hallucinations.

The home team had grown quite hardy to all this, but unfortunately any prospective advantage was severely mitigated by the unfortunate long-term effects of the gas on both players and fans. This was never proved mind, but it was said to cause mood swings, digestive problems and a slow retardation of the frontal lobe. The other negative was the merciless treatment that we received at the hands of the Robins. They were continually tormenting us just because of the fact that the stadium stank like toxic gas. Probably you know the chants and things they goad us with to this very day: 'The club that stinks!' is one, which they always say while pinching their noses at us. And of course, there's the irritating sound of 5,000 idiots in red hissing: 'I can smell GASSSSSS!'

But in the 1970s something incredible happened. The hard-core of fans who stood at the Tote End of the Eastville Stadium were a vigorous mix of punks and greasers, who did their best to counter City at every opportunity they had. The 'Tote Enders' were a creative bunch, coming up with such timeless chants as 'Sh★t fans of a sh★t club with a sh★t mentality!' There are many more gems in the canon, but I need to tell you about the Tote End chant that was to change everything.

Promoted to the second division in 1973/74 season, things were going pretty OK for the Rovers. We were now in the same league as our old arch nemeses down at Ashton Gate. (Which reminds me: 'If I had the wings of a sparrow, if I had the ass of a crow, I'd fly over Ashton tomorrow, and sh★t on the b★★★★★ds below!') Unfortunately, however, the last few derbies had yielded nothing but a run of draws and then a humiliating 2–0 defeat. It was 1975 and the two teams were meeting once more. All right, it wasn't a league match, but it was for the (still very prestigious) Gloucester Cup. Anyway, like every derby, it meant something to all concerned.

After City scored the opener the mood began to sour, and many feared violence. The City fans were giving their usual guff about the gas and the fans in the blue and white began to despair. But just before the end of the first half those legend-ary Tote Enders pulled the cat out of the bag and set it loose among the robins. Out of nowhere they began the (now famous) chant:

> 'We're Gas,
> and we're proud of it,
> we're Gas,

and we're proud of it,
we're Gas,
and we're proud of it,
we're Gas,
and we're proud of it!'

The effect of this was electric. The chant tore around the stadium. The fans were pumping their fists in the air, screaming it at the top of their lungs. We weren't gonna be ashamed any more! We were invincible!! We were THE GAS!!! The enemy simply did not know what to do.

The Eastville gasworks happened to let out a huge payload of noxious gas during the half-time break, a mishap that took place due to an ordinary build-up of pressure that was mishandled by the workmen on duty. The company later offered a routine apology, but such things were not at all an uncommon occurrence. The presence of the gas was tangible to all those in the stadium. It was worse than usual in fact: a real eye-waterer. To the Robins the halftime oranges seemed to taste different somehow, a bit gamey almost – and several of their players reported feeling lightheaded. The Rovers on the other hand, buoyed by their fans' love and pride for the club, stink and all, re-entered the field a changed team. They were now *The Gas*, and proud of it. We went on to win the game 2–1. The genius of the Tote Enders had been to take the stinking truth and turn it into a legend.

It worked a treat. It was shortly after this match that Bristol City began their spectacular decline, becoming the first English club to suffer three relegations on the trot. Lord knows the Rovers have certainly had their downs too, and, of course, fortunes continue to fluctuate all round. However, I like to think that the chant that was born on that bright April afternoon was the trigger for the ensuing downfall of the Robins. Those renowned Tote Enders had officiated at the symbolic inauguration of Bristol City FC's embarrassing 'yo-yo period'.

The Gas name has always been controversial; some Rover fans forever associate it with the derision emanating from Ashton Gate. Certain characters in the Rovers community have fought tooth and nail to eliminate the usage of the term altogether, and ensure that we are known by our 'official' nickname of the Pirates. Personally, when people start talking about 'official nicknames' I always start wondering what's gone wrong with the world. The Pirates is an OK name, I guess. It 'references Bristol's maritime history,' as they say. It is *certainly* better than 'The Robins', a name that fails to conjure any emotion whatsoever, even for City fans. But 'The Gas' is the name with the story.

Anyway, when the Rovers finally moved away from Eastville to Twerton Park in Bath in 1986, God Herself weighed in on the debate. In my view it has been clearly ordained that the Rovers are Gasheads for life. For what was waiting there, just a block or so upwind from the new stadium and clearly visible from the stands? That's right: a gasworks.

THE BUS BOYCOTT

WHAT IS AN 'urban legend'? Many people contend that to be an urban legend, a story must be untrue. You hear people say, 'Oh no, that's not true, it's just an urban legend.' On the other hand, some feel that Bristol's canon of urban legends, far from being a pack of lies, is a sacred treasury of local goings on: the mysteries, comedies and tragedies that unfolded before our eyes and were carefully stored in the collective memory.

In order to settle the question of urban legends, we must first ask, *Who gets to say?* Once we can answer *that* question, we can answer the rest and provide a working definition of the term. During my research I spoke to many people: writers, academics, journalists, collectors of local lore and curios, ghost hunters, raconteurs, tour guides, drunk mums, strange uncles, second cousins once removed, guys-at-the-bar, and many more. For a long time I thought that the answer would be that there is a diversity of equally valid definitions of what an urban legend is, and that we all have a right to say what the term means to us personally. But I was surprised to find out that one particular person's definition is in fact simply *more correct* than any of the others. And, as luck would have it, it's mine.

Firstly, urban legends are stories about *local events* that are at least nominally *true*. You tell them as if they are, or at least could be, true. Secondly, these stories must be in *current circulation*. It is only an urban legend while it is still being told, while it lives in the dream life of the city. That's it. It can be true or false, exaggerated or dumbed down, set in 1992 or Roman times; so long as people are telling it in today's pubs and playgrounds, and telling it like someone believes it, then it is an urban legend.

I say all this to ensure that no one thinks that the inclusion of the following story means that the events described are not true. I know them to be true. That does not stop them being legendary though, does it? This is a tale still told all over the world, for it is a justly famous and important piece of history: the Bristol Bus Boycott.

In the 1960s the Bristol Omnibus Company, owned by the council, did not hire non-white people as conductors or drivers on the buses. This was a perfectly legal policy at the time. People from Bristol's South Asian and West Indian communities could work in the garages, but they could not be seen working on the buses. Management said that it would scare the white workers away and the Transport and General Workers Union agreed with them.

Somehow though, and this bit could be considered a bit confusing, both management and the union were, simultaneously to enforcing this policy of a white-only workforce, claiming that there was no colour bar. 'There is no colour bar,' they said, 'it's just that we happen to bar people of colour.'

Black activists and various people had made a noise about this before. Not least among them was Roy Hackett, legendary community organiser and founder of St Paul's Carnival. But nothing changed, even when the *Bristol Evening Post* ran an exposé on the injustice of the de facto colour bar.

There is a big question about context here. How racist was Bristol in the 1960s? What was it like to live here for West Indians and for Asians during that time? Of course, being a tiny white whippersnapper I can't properly answer that, and so it is beholden on you to go and find some old lady or gent to fill in the blanks. What I will do is tell you some of what I heard for myself. I'll stick to the experience of Jamaicans for a minute. Remember that many of them had not long arrived: the *Windrush* was only a little over a decade previous. It was very hard to find a room in Bristol, due to the fact that many landlords would not hire rooms to black or brown people. Many pubs refused to serve you. So too did some of the shops. There were also violent gangs of Teddy Boys who would chase you through the streets and subject you to horrible beatings or worse.

Still, plenty of Jamaicans who were here during this era have happy memories. I spoke to a man who actually worked for the Bristol Omnibus Company, in the garages mind, all the way through the Boycott era. He and his colleagues, black and white alike, supported the struggle. They also ate and drank and socialised together. He told me that there were those who wanted to judge you or give you a hard time, but he just ignored them. He said he always focused on the positive and didn't want to get down or bitter about people being racist and this and that. The thing about England that really bothered him, he told me with an emphatic nod, was how cold it was! We had a good laugh at that, though the day was actually bright and warm and we were stood relishing it on his front step, a gentle breeze rustling the green beans growing up the house.

But we can't let this man's phenomenal patience and wrought-iron friendliness hide facts salient to the tale: racism was alive and well in every echelon of Bristol society. First off there was the racism we have today, where people are stereotyped according to their culture and race and spend a great deal of time being misunderstood, mistreated and overlooked as a result. In addition to this, there was no legislation against racism, and so whole institutions could be *overtly* exclusionary and prejudiced should they wish to be. The Tory Party, to choose one instance among many, campaigned with racist slogans, and all over our city people were refused entry, or jobs, or common decency because of the colour of their skin.

Things did not change until Paul Stephenson arrived. Here was a black man who was British born and bred. He was from a middle-class home, was well spoken and was highly educated. When Stephenson came to Bristol as a youth worker he quickly learnt about the struggles of black Bristolians: their limited job prospects, their ghettoization in certain areas, and the frosty refusals that greeted them at every turn. Having grown up in England, Stephenson was not as prepared to accept this situation as some of the newer arrivals were. He looked at what Hackett and other activists had been doing, and how they fell into the bus company's denials and excuses like flies into soup. He had an idea.

* * *

Guy Bailey was something of a model citizen. He was upstanding. He had done well in school. He had been an officer in the Boys' Brigade and he was active in church. He was kind, generous and excellent at cricket. He was charming, humble and likeable. A real gent. Paul Stephenson had been waiting for someone just like Guy. Now he had him, and he set the trap. He helped Guy fill out an application to be a conductor. The young man was excited. He knew that to be a bus driver you had to put your time in as a conductor first. He had always been a good driver and he could see himself behind the wheel. He had been to London where many West Indians drove buses, and he fancied he would look pretty right in the uniform once he had it on. Paul did the talking for Guy on the phone, for if they had heard Guy Bailey's Jamaican accent they never would have had him in. Paul had been the only black kid in his class at school and so sounded as white as his peers. Paul charmed the socks off the boss in the phone interview. The man on the other end of the phone was a Mr Cosgrove. He was a tall man with a sandy moustache and an inflated sense of national pride. He saw himself as personable but in fact he was objectionable. He saw himself as a defender of propriety when really he was its destroyer. While he had hardly distinguished himself in the war his self-understanding as a military man had been cemented with unfortunate rigidity.

However, Cosgrove could also fawn over those who stimulated his sense of quality. And so, upon hearing the well-spoken voice and reading the faultless CV, Cosgrove practically begged the nice young man to come in for a face-to-face interview. It was a great relief, expounded Cosgrove to his secretary Martha Thwaite, to have someone of real moral calibre apply for once. The Bristol Omnibus Company was a proud organisation, and they wanted to hire only the cream of the city. They wouldn't take on riff-raff, not while Lt Cosgrove had a say in the matter! The company would fly the flag for the upstanding Britisher even while so many others seemed hell-bent on creating a degenerate society. Martha looked at him coolly while he made this little speech. He suddenly became aware of her gentle lack of interest. She had a way of looking at him that made him most uneasy. Cosgrove cleared his throat, stiffened like someone had pinched his bum, told Martha to alert him when Mr Bailey presented himself, and went back into his office.

And when Mr Bailey did present himself, what a shock Martha got. The story I heard was that she called though to the boss – not taking her eyes off poor Guy for a moment – and stuttered: 'Your appointment's here Mr Cosgrove… but he's black!' The boss, not knowing that he was on speaker and that Bailey could hear every word, said into his phone, 'Tell him all the vacancies are full.'

'But I know they're not full,' Bailey protested. 'Why would you have someone in for an interview when there's no vacancy?'

Injustice is regrettable whenever it occurs, and one of the sad things about the human race is that we consider some people worthy of our sympathy while we ignore the plight of many others. People are fine with bad things happening to people they deem to be bad. This is actually one of the most powerful ways racism operates: pernicious stories cast suspicion on people of colour, criminalising them in the public imagination. Then white people start to lose any qualms they may have had regarding the unequal landscape of privilege in our society, believing that where people are disadvantaged it must be their own fault. Stephenson's genius was precisely the genius of a storyteller: instead of fighting *against* the way we attribute sympathy, he started to work *with* it. He saw the potential for a moving story in the situation, one capable of capturing the hearts of all Bristolians, and it needed only a little help to be told.

Stephenson knew that the image of Cosgrove rejecting someone so obviously capable, kind and reasonable as young Guy Bailey had the power to stir indignation in the most heartless of audiences. Storytelling is the art of directing sympathies, and even if your audience is prejudiced (and of course they always are) a strong tale will have them cheering on their mother-in-laws by the end. Stephenson brought us a masterpiece: short and simple but elegantly constructed and packing tremendous emotional weight. It is a classic of tragedy: *naivety* vs. the *world*. Someone who, from simple goodness, acts as they *should*, vs. someone who cynically hides behind how people *conventionally* act. You must have noticed that kind and reasonable people like Bailey act as if there is hope that the world is a kind and reasonable place, while the unkind and unreasonable despair of it ever being so. *Hope* vs. *Despair*: what more powerful basis is there for a story? And so Stephenson brought Guy's goodness into conflict with the callous racism of the Bristol Omnibus Company.

The architect of the little scene had chosen wisely, for Guy's decency and expectation of decency in return ended up wringing the truth from the boss. Cosgrove had been reduced to coming from his little office and standing behind his secretary's chair to address Mr Bailey. Against the young man's questions Cosgrove found himself helpless. He had purposefully stood behind Martha because he did not want her to be able to look at him as he spoke. Martha herself was paralysed. She could see that Bailey was wronged and cringed for Cosgrove as he desperately tried not to mention the unofficial colour-bar.

'Well I don't understand. If you have the job then why not try me for it? I am a very hard worker Mr Cosgrove,' explained Bailey.

Cosgrove moved his mouth a few times. His moustache twitched like it was considering jumping off his face. Then he slouched a little as he crumbled and admitted the truth. 'There's no point in you coming in to interview. We don't hire your sort…' Cosgrove's voice trailed off in a pathetic stutter: 'I mean… you people.'

Stephenson had a journalist from the *Post* speak to Guy right after the horrible little episode, while it was still raw. In the world of story it is enough to have just one Little Red Riding Hood, but in real life you need two or three victims before people start to recognise the Wolf. And so Stephenson told the tale again. The next young man he sent had a photographer from the *Post* in tow. And after that he sent someone else, and so on and on. Stephenson was making it impossible for Cosgrove to tell if the people he was sending were black, and they were all model candidates in every other way. The company's rejection of them gave human faces to the victims of the policy, and, as the story took hold, more and more people joined the boycott of bus services that Stephenson and other activists were advising.

There were marches. Tony Benn, MP for Bristol South East, gave his support, as did the Labour leader Harold Wilson MP. Bailey was a great personality for the whole campaign, because it was impossible to not be on this guy's side. Who would want to travel with a bus company that would turn up its nose at a top bloke like Guy Bailey? More Bristolians were behind him every day. He became a symbol of everything that was human and decent in our city, not to mention a hero for refusing to accept injustice. However, Guy himself was not sure about all the attention. He never signed up for this. He was just trying to get a job. And now he was at the centre of a campaign that was attracting attention from international media, with people drawing comparisons with the civil rights struggles going on in the southern USA. Listening to great stories is a great comfort, to be sure, but to be a character *living* such a story is a very exhausting business indeed.

Nevertheless, Stephenson, Hackett and other activists were making hay while the sun was shining. They were sitting outside the depots and stopping the buses from leaving. White people were starting to get onside. White mums on the school run would drop the kids off and then come and join the pickets. It was a first time most of them had ever spoken to a West Indian. And they were finding out that they were alright.

The Transport and General Workers' Union (TGWU) were losing the support of almost everyone. They were condemned by other trade unions for helping to oppress those who should be their comrades. They lost a libel case brought by Stephenson after they tried to besmirch his good name. The bus company was faring even worse. The city had turned against it. Those who could not observe the boycott because the buses were too vital to them would torment the drivers. 'If you were black I bet you'd have been on time...' they'd tease. And worst of all, the riders dropped the customary 'Cheers drive!' that every Bristolian is duty-bound to intone as he or she hops off a bus.

It was too much for all concerned, and on the very same day that Martin Luther King Jr. stood on the steps of the Lincoln Memorial and made his 'I have a dream' speech, the TGWU voted to support the hiring of black conductors and drivers. The Bristol Omnibus Company soon followed suit.

A certain Mr Raghbir Singh was the first non-white applicant to be accepted. And soon he was donning the distinctive brown uniform of the Bristol Omnibus Company and proudly sporting a matching turban. Guy Bailey did not apply again. He felt crushed by the experience and sought alternative employment.

A few short years after the victory, in 1965, Labour got back into government. One of the first things that the new Prime Minister Harold Wilson did was to pass the Race Relations Act. Ever since then, discrimination in public places and in employment has been illegal. It is well known that the change in law was directly inspired by the Bristol campaign's success and popularity. As well as striking a blow against institutional racism, the activists at the heart of the events in the city gave Bristol a new story to tell, one in which individuals of colour, for the first time, were in the driver's seat. Bailey, Hackett and Stephenson have been beloved personalities about town ever since, and in recognition of what they had done for the city and the country, the three of them were awarded an OBE apiece by the Queen herself.

Sure, a few bigoted drivers quit in protest, and Cosgrove soon retired in a huff to bully his wife (and once she left him, to inflict his personality on various neighbours) – but the majority of the workers at the company welcomed their new colleagues, as did the passengers. Soon every stop on every route was once again punctuated by rounds of 'Cheers drive! Cheers drive! Cheers drive!' And with this little nicety reinstated, all was relatively well in Bristol town.

THE HOTWELLS CROCODILE AND OTHER BEASTS

Crocodile #1

My friends, a word of advice: to tell an urban legend to maximum effect you have to take your time. Don't rush it. Locate the moment of drama – whether it's an encounter with terror or a tearful reunion – and savour it. Your audience won't complain if you take a bit of licence with a scene or two. Remember that, sometimes, in order to best get across the truth of an event, to most accurately express what it was like to be there, you have to jig things around a bit. OK, maybe the fish wasn't exactly '*this* big', but it *was* big, and the best way to communicate the thrill of hauling a big fish from the water is to hold your hands far enough apart so your interlocutor can get a handle on that feeling. It is the job of a tape measure to communicate the size of the fish; your job is to communicate the size of the experience. Turning events into stories involves some work on presentation. When you sense a dramatic scene twinkling in a tale, don't leave it half obscured: take it up, polish it, and hold it up to the light. This is all exaggeration is really: a proper appreciation of reality.

I think most people sense this and need no special encouragement. Thus, people have taken their time when they've recounted to me what they know of Jolyon Rea. In most versions of the tale, his bus screeches to a halt on Bedminster Bridge and he leaps out, pointing into the water and screaming about a crocodile. Paying no mind to the beeping traffic building behind the bus, or the passengers clutching their handbags and tutting, or texting their complaints to Wessex Connect, Jolyon jumped up and down trying to get everyone to see what he saw. But the clever croc only grinned at him and slipped below the surface of the water.

But this is not what happened. And to be honest with you, if spinning a good yarn involves besmirching the reputation of an honest man then I'm not interested. The joke's over I'm afraid. Jolyon is no loop-de-loop. I'm going to tell this story joylessly if I have to. It is not important that you appreciate the high emotion of Jolyon's sighting. I'm sure that you can appreciate what it would be like to suddenly see a crocodile in the Avon: surprising. Very surprising. Exaggeration here would only confuse the issue. Particularly considering Jolyon's remarkable sanity and restraint in the circumstances. We've all had our fun with this story, but what matters here is that you appreciate the facts. For I tell you now: Jolyon Rea was telling the truth.

Jolyon actually saw the beast in his wing mirror as he was crossing over the Avon at Bedminster roundabout. The traffic was thick so he had time to get a nice long gander. He had seen crocodiles and alligators in the wild in Florida, so he knew what he was looking at. Its back legs and tail were on the muddy bank, and it was just slinking off into the water. Jolyon's few passengers were all listening to devices so he couldn't get their attention. He very calmly drove his route until he could safely stop the bus. At this point he hailed an officer of the law and notified her about what he had seen. One of the things you should note about Jolyon is his persistence in the face of adversity. The police laughed – at first, at least – and of course since that day Jolyon has faced the mickey at work on a daily basis. The whole city seemed to laugh or shake its head at him at one point. But through all this the man has stuck to his story. He is not mad. He even underwent a voluntary drug test to show he hadn't been high on the wacky stuff at the time of the sighting. In actual fact, I have it on good authority that it was his clear sanity and dogged refusal to drop his testimony that finally meant the police started to take what he had seen seriously.

First the police contacted Bristol Zoo, who, after doing a slightly panicked recount, reported that all their large reptiles were accounted for. They suggested the beast could have escaped from Noah's Arc Zoo, where (so they claimed) security can be lax – but when contacted the Arc denied it and said it sounded like one of Bristol's. Next the police began a thorough search of the Avon, led by the very capable Sergeant Markus Brund. This could well have yielded results, but Brund and his colleagues broke it off to rush to Eastville Park, where they had received reports of another sighting. Brund is a cautious man, and he is not going to place any of his officers in danger just to save face or money. For this reason, he had the PCs search the park dressed in full riot gear. You can't be too careful, especially when there is a large man-eating reptile on the loose. However, unfortunately for Brund, not to mention the people of Bristol, the sighting in Eastville Park turned out to be a hoax. Two teenage boys had dressed up in a home-made suit and were splashing around in the water just down from Snuff Mills. The suit was apparently quite impressive, but it didn't receive as much attention as the image of Sergeant Brund and the PCs garbed in full riot gear poking around in shrubberies. The ensuing Twitter storm was so fierce and derogatory to the constabulary's professionalism that the investigation was pulled.

However, sightings kept being reported. The second proper one was just a day or so later. Kelly Gray, a bookkeeper from Southville, was on her way home. She was in the car and singing along to Meatloaf (I assume) when she saw the beast. She was just on the approach to the Bedminster Bridge Roundabout and it was down under the bridge, swimming slickly through the muddy water more or less exactly where Jolyon had seen it. She almost crashed the car. On reaching home she told her mum, who convinced her to inform the authorities. She was scared of the inevitable ridicule, but she wanted to do the right thing before someone got hurt.

Knowing what we know now it seems incredible that the search was called off and this whole thing became a matter for japes, silly memes and witty banter. Even the police were guilty of getting involved in this, with the Tweets emanating from the social media team growing distinctly jocular, much to the chagrin of sensible Sergeant Brund and several concerned police divers. The latter knew Bristol's complex waterways better than anybody and understood how easily a large aquatic reptile could hide itself. Brund and the diving faction still very much wanted to be able to pronounce these waterways safe – something they could only do in good conscience after conducting a proper search.

But the constabulary would devote no more resources to the matter, notwithstanding the fact that crocodiles are notoriously fond of human flesh; killing around 30 per cent of some people in places such as Australia's Northern Territory. Remember, everyone who *actually* saw the beast was terrified and contacted the police. But the more the reports flooded in, the more they were discredited. Something about unusual testimony means it is easily disbelieved when there is lots of it. The testimony of a single person may be listened to, but the testimony of many is routinely ignored. Much of human life in a globalised world involves ignoring most of what other people experience, and as a consequence we have become excellent at dismissing in bulk all testimony that happens to challenge our assumptions.

When it comes to the photographs, I have to say that I myself dismissed them at first because of their extreme similarity to logs. However, after the recent revelation from Chew Magna, I went back and looked at them again. They do look like logs, that's true, but consider this impression from an evolutionary perspective. Crocodiles are old. They are actually *dinosaurs that have remained unchanged for millions of years*. They have survived by laying low; they count on not being seen.

They have had over 80 million years to practise this and they are very, very good at it. If you've ever gone out looking for them in the wild you will know how hard it is to spot them. If you went crocodile spotting in the Everglades one day and you didn't see one, you wouldn't conclude that they didn't exist. So why do this in the Avon? One of the main ways in which crocodiles and alligators hide is to look like logs. They can look like logs even whilst moving at speed through the water. They have evolved to look like logs. It is hardly surprising that when we look at one, we think that it looks a lot like a log.

As far as we know, no Bristolian has yet been hurt. The reptile handlers up at the Zoo suspect that the beast has been living on a diet of waterfowl supplemented by fish. Technically speaking, all swans belong to the Queen, so she will doubtless soon want to know why the Bristol establishment didn't take threats to her property more seriously. For now, the self-satisfied smiles of those who quaffed and sniggered at tales of the beast are rapidly fading in the face of potent new evidence that the Bristol crocodile lives.

The Coronation Chicken

Folk did not always believe in the Coronation Chicken (CC) either, but it eventually made itself impossible to disbelieve. It viciously attacked literally hundreds of people over a period of perhaps twenty years, from the late 1980s until sometime in the early naughties. For those who don't know it, this beast was a huge, wild cock that roamed Bedminster at night. No one knew where CC roosted, but it would often attack solitary walkers walking along Coronation Road. Because these people were alone and usually drunk, no one believed them. It is not known why the chicken attacked, although having heard a few first-hand accounts it seems likely that these assaults were actually a string of muggings. Think about it: drunk people are often eating chips or a kebab. If you run toward them, squawking and flapping your wings, or if you jump out of tree and claw at their hats with your sharp talons, they tend to drop their food and run. Then you can eat the food. Simple. Eventually the evidence piled up, and there were just so many people from Bedminster arriving home with scratches and peck marks that they could no longer be explained away as secret affairs. Some say that a Bedmo residents' group hired a vigilante hunter to kill the bird, and eventually had the thing served up at a street party on Raleigh Road. They made CC into Coronation Chicken (how could they not) and the thing was so large that it filled over 200 tasty sandwiches. Others, of course, claim that the fowl beast is still very much on the loose.

Mixu the Chicken

Mixu was a wild chicken who lived at the Three Lamps Junction on the Wells Road during the 1990s. There are actually some reports of this chicken being violent too, although accusations like this do tend to spring up around religious leaders, even when they are entirely innocent. This is on account of the fact that the human psyche is so thoroughly traumatised and acculturated to negativity that when we encounter the divine, or even just positive thinking, we unconsciously begin to try to smother it with filth. Once we have safely discredited or destroyed it we can keep calm and carry on with miserable-as-usual. Now, I never actually met Mixu, but if even half the things they say about her are true then we are talking about a creature who saw further than others do, and not just because she lived on a hill.

She was a wild thing, but remarkably unafraid. She would spend her days standing on the steps beneath the Three Lamps watching the world go by. One night, three students were making their way up the hill from a night out at the Oceana nightclub. Only when they knelt before the steps did they realise that indeed she had been calling them. These students became her first human followers, and thereafter they were heard to say 'Verily, whosoever should sit at the foot of the Three Lamps will be HER disciple.'

This is what I heard: Mixu preferred not to be a one-woman egg machine. She preferred not to live in a box. She preferred not to be impregnated. She preferred not to have any male chicks born to her thrown in a blender. And so Mixu had escaped. She had seen the door of the warehouse open and she simply walked towards the light. The little rectangle became a big rectangle, and thereafter the world.

Mixu's followers called her the Daughter of the World, because she was hatched from the injustice of the present system. She came to bring balance between the creatures of Totterdown. The pigeons liked her. The rats were devoted and brought a surfeit of food. The students made a beautiful, lo-fi GeoCities website for her – but for most human beings Mixu was nothing but a novelty.

In the winter of 1999, some of her followers rushed Mixu up to the Avon Lodge Veterinary Group. She died shortly after arriving. They found enough rat poison in her belly to kill her a hundred times over.

Crocodile #2

In the summer of 2017 a pair of experienced water engineers were doing some routine work at Chew Valley Reservoir, which is Bristol's major water source. It was a regular day at work for Wadia Mirza and Osod Begenblossoms, when suddenly they spotted, sunbathing on the concrete bank, what looked like a baby alligator or crocodile. Picture the scene: for a moment Wadia and Osod are frozen, the breeze mutters in the bulrushes. Then, a nervous flick of the tail on the crocodile's part starts Osod moving towards it, crouched low and hands outstretched. Of course, as soon as it senses him coming, the little beast starts scampering along the concrete towards the safety of the lake. It reaches the edge and leaps gracefully into the water, only to re-emerge a second later trapped in a net on a long pole. Moving quickly, Wadia had grabbed the net from the top of the van and managed to cut off the crocodile's escape just in time. The RSPCA were called, and the beast was given over to an expert handler.

The boffins soon identified the animal as a caiman, which is neither crocodile nor alligator but rather another species in the ancient order of the Crocodilia. Of course, it doesn't take an expert to figure out that where there is a baby, there is a mother; and that where there is a mother, there is a father. The following morning, in Bridewell Police Station, Sergeant Markus Brund slammed his fist down on his desk in a moment of uncharacteristic anger. In front of him his browser showed the news on the BBC website. Had people listened in the first place then the police maybe could have cleared the issue up with minimum fuss. Now they are breeding. Now Bristol has a rapidly expanding population of caimans to worry about. And all because people assume that beast stories are necessarily fictional.

5
ALFRED THE GORILLA

SOMETIME IN THE early 2000s, a man lay dying. In his final hour he requested the presence of a priest so that he could confess his sins before he passed on. He was not a religious man, but there was something he did not want to take with him to the grave. The tale he told stunned the poor old priest, who that night could not resist telling his wife. The wife could not resist telling Sally, and, well, Sally likes a bit of gossip, and so here we are in a book of urban legends.

So, what had the confessor unburdened himself of? Well, he had admitted to a crime that had remained unsolved for forty years: it was he who had stolen Alfred the Gorilla, the beloved 'Dictator of Bristol Zoo'.

* * *

The year: 1925. The place: thick jungle in the Belgian Congo. A pair of gorillas are hunted through the forest. They have been raiding the farmer's field for food and now the farmer wants rid of them. He tracks them though the trees, holding a rifle in his warm hands. He stops, shoots. A mighty beast falls to the forest floor. Its mate, the female, cannot resist stopping. She moves back, stretching out her fingers and gently touching her companion's face. The farmer has reloaded the rifle. He shoots. The gorilla's body barely jolts with the bullet's entry. She looks at the farmer, trying to decide whether to charge or flee. Her body is in shock. The farmer reloads, shoots.

Somewhere on the mountain of black fur, a baby is cling-ing. The farmer spots it and takes it home to his wife. She has just had a baby herself. She takes the little creature and looks at it. The faces of gorillas read like human faces. She is hold-ing the gorilla baby and smiling. She suckles it as if it was her own. It grows.

Of course, it is very tame indeed. And, of course, it's cute. The family love it. The village loves it. It grows. And grows.

And grows. The family are struggling to feed it. The farmer says it must go. His wife and son are tearful but they take it to the market. A tame gorilla is a rare thing. They sell it to a Greek merchant. He's usually on the lookout for stones to take back to Europe, but he's an opportunist. He buys a teenaged gorilla. He names him Augustine. Augustine is a fast learner. The Greek teaches him to separate the real rubies from the fake, to tell when someone is lying, the taste of raw gold in water.

The pair travel on to Mbalmayo in Cameroon. An eccentric Italian nobleman pays a great deal of money for Augustine after seeing him walk sedately through the streets on an errand. The Greek is sorry to part with his friend. He shares the money with him 50/50, after taking back what he paid in the first place. He is a merchant, after all. The two shake hands and Augustine turns to leave with the Italian. On the boat back to Italy the gorilla spends his time looking out over the water at the continent they are leaving. His name is changed to Alfonso. He does not mind.

Alfonso lives in Italy. He lives the highlife, meeting all the most disreputable nobles and going to all the most debauched parties. He frequents Rome, Napoli, Milano, Turin – a hundred manor houses and grand estates. Luxury hotels and grand balls. He dresses in a cravat. He smokes. He swings from chandeliers. But he's playing to the crowd, and when he gets lost by his master in a game of cards, he does not mind.

The chap who has won him is very happy. He is a ruddy-faced, lucky gentleman from a merry town in the west of England. When they get home, the man takes the gorilla for a walk upon the Downs. A chill rain falls. The gorilla pulls his coat about him. They stand by the observatory and look out over the Avon Gorge. The man asks the gorilla if he would like an English name. The gorilla looks at him. The man dubs him Alfred.

'Follow me old chap, I want to show you something.'

Alfred follows. They walk through the Downs until they get to the zoo. The two pay the entry charge and go in. In those days the animals in the zoo were freer than they are today, and often walked abroad looking at the people. Alfred and the man sit on a bench and have an ice cream. They watch the lemurs playing with a little human. 'I wondered if you'd be happier here, Alfred?'

Alfred looks around. He sees group of parakeets nesting in a tree. They're gossiping with a giraffe as she eats. Some meerkats sprint by on an inscrutable errand. The parrots are teaching some children to swear. Alfred nods. He reaches for his purse to pay the man what he is worth. 'No no! Don't be silly. I wouldn't dream of it. I'll let the zoo know you're here.'

Alfred ponders the word 'zoo'. Soon he comes to understand. The accommodation is basic but adequate. The food is simple but nourishing. The keepers do not accept any money for rent or meals. You are treated well. But you cannot leave. When Alfred walks to the door they are always there to stop him. They shake their heads and wave their hands, smiling apologetically. Alfred can see they are scared of him. He does not want to scare anybody.

Frank and Bert work in the zoo. They are nice guys. Alfred doesn't want to scare anybody. This is a cold country. He has nowhere to go. Frank gives Alfred a jumper. Bert gives him a hat. They all laugh when Alfred wears the hat. It is the hat that an entertainer wears. The people who come to the zoo like Alfred. Every day children ask, 'How long till we get to see Alfie?'

Alfred is friends with his keeper, Mustafa. Mustafa has a moustache. He is from Cyprus. In England he calls himself Max. In the winter, Max and Alfred sit in Alfred's enclosure and have a mug of cocoa, maybe a cheeky cigarette, although officially Alfred has given up. This is a cold country.

Outside the walls of the zoo something is happening. Down the hill, over the centre where the trams ring their bells, up to Old Market, and beyond, there is unrest. The unemployed riot. People are hungry. The socialists rout the fascist Black Shirts out of Knowle West after three days of fighting. The police quell protests with their truncheons.

The people love Alfred. They all want to shake his hand. The children want to stroke his hair. For some reason this makes him sad. But he lets them. There is a new director of the zoo. He has a beard.

There is a war in Europe. Britain is in a state of war. Max is gone. Nobody tells Alfred why.

The animals spend more time locked up in their cages. It is a time of war. People are scared.

Every night the air-raid siren sings a bad song. Every night planes fly over. Every night you can hear bombs exploding in the city below.

One day Alfred is walking around the zoo, thinking his thoughts. A photographer takes a picture of him. Alfred will consent to have his picture taken if: a) there is good light, b) he looks nice that day, and c) his permission is sought. The criteria were not fulfilled. Alfred wants the man to destroy the film. The man has a beard. He doesn't understand. Alfred slaps the camera from his hand and smashes it.

Alfred is locked in his enclosure all the time. Alfred becomes grumpy. He hates bearded men. He throws his poop at bearded men. He pees on people. He hates the sound of aeroplanes. He screams at them. He screams very, very loudly. He can tell people are scared. They are scared of the planes and they are scared of Alfred the Gorilla. This makes him sad. And yet still he screams at the planes.

The people of Bristol love Alfred. They love him more than they love anyone. He is the most popular creature in the city. They jokingly call him 'The Dictator of Bristol Zoo'. He is famous across the whole country. Soldiers take pictures of Alfred the Gorilla with them to war. Looking at him gives them a laughing courage. Alfred knows that pictures are important.

Alfred is grumpy. He hates bearded men. He throws poop at people. He pees on people. He shouts at planes. Alfred also hates the elephant. Because she is sleepy and docile, she is still allowed to walk around the zoo. Alfred misses Max. Alfonso misses the good times. Augustine misses the Greek. The baby misses his mum and his brother. A gorilla misses the Congo and the dead parents that he never knew.

Alfred is grumpy. He only likes children and sparrows. The sparrows sit upon his fat forefinger. The children come and sit and point. He tells them a story with his eyebrows. He tells them about how he was lost in a game of cards, even though he himself had quit while he was ahead. The children laugh and point. He touches his fingers to theirs.

The Blitz has finished. Many people have gone to war. Alfred lets an exhausted mother sleep while he watches the baby in the perambulator. St Augustine wrote that if a human baby is not sinful, it is not for want of trying. The circumstances under which the baby will not cry are few. One of them is if a gorilla should jump up and down, grinning and grinning and grinning. Alfred's face hurts.

Alfred gets sick, Alfred gets well. One day, Alfred throws his poop and it goes right in a man's beard.

Alfred is not unhappy. The war goes on. The Blitz has stopped, but now the doodlebugs come. They go whirring and whining across the sky. Then they go silent. Then they go *Wooomph*.

Alfred wants to escape. He will leave at night, walk south. He will commandeer a fishing boat. He will sail over the Channel, round the coast of France, down past Portugal, past Tangier, being careful not to crash into the Rock of Gibraltar. Then into the Mediterranean. He will sail to Cyprus and try and find Max. Someone will know where he is, among his people. Max was raised by his grandmother. Perhaps he has escaped the human war and is already there. Max will come with Alfred. They can sail up the Nile Delta. Up the Nile. They will travel on. Alfred can protect Max. The desert might be tricky. Max is not stupid. They will get to the forest. The forest presses in on your ears, your nose, your eyes, your fur, your tongue, your heart. He will take Max to his human mother. 'Mum, this is Max. Max has a moustache.'

The sparrows nest in Alfred's enclosure. The people of Bristol love Alfred. They have pictures of him. He no longer cares about photographers taking pictures. Even when he sleeps. Everything happens whether you feel ready for it or not. Don't cry little baby: watch my dance. The people of Bristol love Alfred the Gorilla. The war continues. There is not much food. The people are hungry. The animals are hungrier. The zoo needs the people of Bristol. The zoo needs Alfred.

The Home Guard is stationed in Bristol Zoo. Alfred hates their guts for some reason. They are scared of Alfred. They stop marching and walk normally when they pass his cage. They have bad dreams about a bomb releasing him. Bad dreams where Alfred is free.

More and more planes go over the zoo. Alfred screams. The monkeys scream. The hyenas laugh. A wolf howls. Even the elephant makes an elephant noise. Alfred screams. Alfred is sick. Alfred's scream is hoarse. He coughs. The planes drone overhead, carrying bombs or carrying men. Alfred screams. The people of Bristol say the planes are killing him. Alfred hates planes, buses, soldiers, bearded men and the elephant. Alfred has tuberculosis.

After Alfred dies, Bristol mourns. They have him stuffed. Alfred is kept in the museum. The people of Bristol love Alfred the Gorilla.

* * *

There is a story from Bristol aquarium about an octopus who was very good at escaping. Octopuses are living brains. Each of their eight legs is a leg of brain. This octopus, Sandra, was particularly clever. She always found a way to escape. She escaped eleven times, each time breaking into another tank and eating a different fish. Swimming down the corridor of the aquarium at night was like walking through St Nick's Market choosing what to have for lunch. Sandra would let herself back into her tank after she'd had a good feed. The head of the aquarium wants to know where the expensive fish are off to. She has all employees questioned. She has her suspicions.

Then one night they see Sandra on the CCTV. They put a breezeblock on the top of her tank. Sandra wants to escape. She sits and watches. Her head billows as she thinks.

One day an intern leaves the block a little bit off after feeding. Sandra can see her talking to someone, not paying attention to the task. She is stupid and weak. This is what Sandra has been waiting for. That night, she crouches at the top of the tank. She grips on hard. She goes *Thwack! Thwack! Thwack!* against the door with one leg, two legs, three legs. The block shifts a little each time. Sandra can see it poking over the edge of the tank. She pushes, the brick slides. *Crack!* onto the stone floor it falls. Someone is watching. Sandra can hear footsteps running. A light is flashing. Sandra climbs out of her tank. She is holding her breath. The footsteps are thumping. She waits against the wall. The door flies open, squashing her against the wall. She grips onto it, holding it open. A man has run to her tank. He is shining a light on the fallen block. He is stupid and weak. Sandra slips around the door and it swings shut behind her. There is a drain before her. An octopus can fit through small gaps for they have no bones. The man shines his light on her. Sandra is shiny. She is holding her breath. She falls through the gap, through the darkness, and into water. She breathes. Sandra is free.

* * *

Alfred has stood in Bristol Museum, by the café, since 1948. Except, that is, for three days in 1956, when he was somewhere else. One morning the cleaner came to give the old gorilla his daily dusting, and he could not help but notice that he was gone. He looked left and right, but there was no gorilla. He was scared because he was the only one in the museum and Alfred is the favourite exhibit of the people of Bristol. He will be accused.

There is an investigation. The cleaner clutches his cap in his hands and rubs his bald head with worry. Bristol Museum suspects a communist plot. The gorilla is missing. Everyone in Bristol is talking about it. Where can he have gone? Who would steal Alfred? The children cry when they see the empty stand. The newspaper writes Alfred's second obituary.

But then, after three days, Alfred is back on his stand. Alfred went away and came back. The people of Bristol love Alfred the Gorilla.

* * *

Sometime in the early 2000s, a man lay dying. In the final hour, he requested the presence of a priest so that he could confess his sins before he passed on. Many years ago, when he was still a young man, he had stolen Alfred the Gorilla.

There is a classic type of urban legend, versions of which everyone everywhere seem to tell. It nearly always stars students, but it would work with any revellers really. These revellers have a penchant for stealing exotic things during their all-night drinking sessions. I've heard tell about penguins in bathtubs and tiger cubs in handbags. These stories are often set in 'Rag Week' and so I've come to call them Rag Week stories. They are not great stories, and I was loath to include any here. Apart from anything else, they just seem so made up. But then there was Alfred. Alfred was genuinely stolen by some drunken students during Rag Week. Presumably there was a bet or a dare. These students had discovered the tunnels and catacombs that run beneath the city of Bristol. They worked out how to get from an out-of-the-way basement in the university into the museum.

On the night of the crime these students were drunk. Very drunk. Upon seeing they had Alfred the Gorilla in the living room they quickly closed the curtains. The party went on. It was Rag Week after all. Alfred wore a cravat. He smoked. He lived the highlife. He was playing to the crowd. It was just like old times. But when his new friends saw the state that Bristol was in, they felt bad. There was crying in the streets. Children were inconsolable. A housewife in Totterdown threatened to kill herself if Alfred wasn't returned. The students felt bad and scared. They decided to take Alfred back. In the dead of night, they wrapped him in a sheet and took him back through the tunnels and into the museum.

Alfred still resides there today. He is a bit grumpy, and yet something of an entertainer. He has been caged and he has been free. He likes children and sparrows. He dislikes planes and beards. People stop to point and stare or to say hello. An old man with a moustache and a tear in his eye. The people of Bristol love Alfred the Gorilla.

CLIFTON SUSPENSION BRIDGE STORIES

Bridge Jump #1

When it comes to sharing stories of Clifton Suspension Bridge, no one ever talks about the American Laurence Donovan. Unfortunately, this means I cannot rightly include the tale here, for the good people at The History Press were keen to make sure that this book included only those tales that Bristolians are still telling today. A historian or a folklorist may go to the library or the archive, but the storyteller listens in the pubs and the playgrounds. I've spent many hours up at Clifton Suspension Bridge itself, questioning visitors, or eavesdropping as people share stories over sandwiches and ice creams, and I've never heard anyone mention old Lorry Donovan. As far as oral history goes, he's a nonentity: dropped completely from the collective memory. No matter. It's a small loss, for the man was very likely a fraud. You see, from his arrival in our town, self-styled 'daredevil' Donovan was boasting that he could survive the jump from Brunel's famous gorge-straddling masterpiece. He claimed to have successfully jumped from New York City's Brooklyn Bridge in 1886. Not sure if this is true or not, but either way, Brooklyn Bridge has only a piddling 41-metre plunge to the water while Clifton Suspension Bridge boasts a gert 75 metres.

Of course, it didn't take Bristolians too long to demand that Donovan either prove his mettle and jump or shut up about bridges altogether. To his credit, he accepted the dare with a flourish. A date was fixed, 22 June 1887, and Donovan spent the next few weeks happily promoting his coming escapade. However, I'm sorry to report that he proved a real disappointment to the crowds who showed up on the appointed day. The little performance was going well at first. Donovan was there, dressed in some alarming knickerbockers, pacing up and down along the middle of the bridge with all the agitation and pomp of a bird of paradise. After a bit of this he would stop to limber up. He stretched this way and that, throwing some very pretty contortions. It was a convincing little sequence and some of those assembled even started to believe that he might just know what he is doing. But then each time he stood on the barrier and looked down toward the muddy vein of Avon far below he found he needed to start his warm-up routine from the top. This carried on for a while, and truth be told it became embarrassing. In the end the police arrested him and, reading the sources, I am still not quite sure if this was: a) for his own safety, b) because they pitied him and wanted to give him a chance to save face, or c) just to salvage some kind of spectacle for the hundred or so Bristolians who had trudged up to Clifton Suspension Bridge eagerly expecting a dramatic death.

Several nights later, however, in a much less publicised event, Donovan seemingly achieved the jump. Witnesses say his body looked remarkably stiff as it plummeted down the gorge and slapped into the river. Well, his associates did retrieve him dripping from the muck, and this much at least was witnessed by some generally reliable dog walkers. They took him straight up to the Bristol Royal Infirmary for a once-over. The nurse who administered the medical apparently reported that he had an impressive bruise upon his backside. However, it was not one gained, in her professional opinion, 'from jumping off that there bridge'.

Brunel's Delight Extended

Of course, everyone knows that it was Isambard Kingdom Brunel who designed Clifton Suspension Bridge, but it's not everyone who knows that the diminutive Bristolian still haunts the place today. However, the story is told sufficiently frequently – even if mainly in monotones by long-suffering tour guides – that it deserves a place in these pages. Typically for little Brunel, who always liked to get high on his own supply so to speak, he is still sometimes caught in the act of admiring his handiwork. You must have heard that the sunrise can only be viewed from inside his famous railway tunnel at Box on his birthday, 9 April. And why begrudge the engineer such a flourish if he has the skill to pull it off? You wouldn't get it these days. These days we've risk assessments instead of flourish. He was a rare one, Brunel, and it's a rare thing he made, the bridge across the gorge. It's become the enduring symbol of our city. And so who can blame the ghost for wandering its length of an evening? You see, the poor man died of a stroke before it was ever finished, and so his shade dallies here on earth and admires the finished product at its leisure. You'll know when he's there because you'll smell tobacco smoke up at the viewing point by the observatory, though you be all alone and fastidiously health-conscious yourself. That, or you'll hear his footsteps, slow and steady, coming towards you over the bridge.

The Slide

One thing that I wanted to know more about regarding Clifton Suspension Bridge was the rock slide. For those who don't know it, it is giant face of flat stone that lies at a convenient angle to slide down. Of course, all day every day the thing is chock-a-block with sliding children, and the odd adult who goes down is shocked at the speed and danger of it. The remarkable thing is that while there is a kind of channel that has been worn smooth by generations of children, everywhere else (where the rock is in its original condition) is too coarse to slide down. This means, if you think about it, that at some point all of it was once too coarse to slide down.

Now, remember this slide is not an 'official' thing. It is not managed, or even condoned, by any official body – at least not anybody over the age of 12. The council haven't yet attempted to prevent people sliding there, but certainly they will be thinking about it. Everyone can tell that the slide was made *by* children, *for* children. Children don't have access to industrial floor sanders, or whatever else it would take to carve out a slidey channel from coarse rock. The conclusion is obvious: at some point in history some children heroically scraped and bumped their way down a bad slide. These children (Edwardian? Medieval? Roman?) ripped their pants and scraped their backsides to start the process of slidification. It doesn't sound too likely does it? My old mum tells me it was already smooth in the 1950s, when she started sliding down it. Being raised Catholic, my mum couldn't help but point out the similarity of the slide to the foot of the statue of St Peter in his Basilica in Rome. So many centuries of pilgrims have kissed this statue's right foot that it has been worn smooth as a polished pebble. Yes Mum, but the difference is that even in the beginning the foot was pretty kissable. The slide, on the other hand, cannot have been slide-able for the first hundred years or so. It is a mystery that so many children could have been so selflessly forward thinking – not something those little guys are particularly famed for. Interested in this puzzle, I went up to the slide and tried to talk to some of the sliders about it. They all blanked me and continued on with their relentless sliding – some going down on their backs, some on their fronts, and some even trying to stand up and slide down on their socks. They were prepared to discuss which clothing types achieved the fastest top speeds, the various ways of connecting to fellow sliders fore and aft to make a train, how many goes it is possible to get out of 'one more go', and a multitude of other points relating to form and technique, but none were in the slightest bit interested in the mysterious origins of the slide itself. Eventually, a little ginger-haired boy with a sympathetic look on his face came up to me, shaking his head and saying, 'It's just for fun mister, it's just for fun…'

Bridge Jump #2

If there is one story about the bridge that really demands a place here, it is that of Sarah Ann Henley and the events of 1885. Now, not *everyone* knows this one already, but enough have told it over the years to carry it safely down the generations to my ear. Some stories are bulky and unassailable; for instance the life stories of the greats, like Joan of Arc or Robin Hood. These are tales that crash down the ages like tanks through scrubland. Ironic, isn't it, that so often these individuals struggled to be heard or even just left alone to live in their own lifetimes, but ever since they popped their clogs their fans have eagerly girded their stories until they are unstoppable. But the story I am about to tell you is quite different from monoliths such as these. It is one of those that at any point could have been quashed, forgotten, or trodden like a leaf into the autumn mud. I like to call this type *survivor stories*, just on account of how they could so easily have been forgotten. They're local interest stories, really, and are hard-pressed to persist in a global age. Somehow though, you'll find that the odd one – despite not starring anyone of remarkable insight, bravery or intelligence; despite the story itself not being especially epic or wise or hilarious or tragic; even though it be but a minor tale, hopelessly provincial in scope – has fluttered down through the generations and landed in your lap.

The year was 1885. Sarah Ann Henley was a 22-year-old woman with a romantic sensibility, sturdy knees and a square, pretty face. Sarah was an Easton girl, but worked in the Rising Sun out in Ashton. I'd wager that if you went in there on a quiet afternoon (perhaps just for a quick one after you'd been walking the dog in Greville Smyth Park), you would find her cleaning a glass and singing 'The Blacksmith' or some other soppy ballad to herself. She was just that way inclined. Folk look for different things in this world, and Sarah was one of those souls who was looking for love.

> *A blacksmith courted me,*
> *Nine months and better,*
> *He fairly won my heart,*
> *Wrote me a letter.*
> *With his hammer in his hand,*
> *He looked so clever,*
> *And if I was with my love.*
> *I would live forever.*

Well, there was a boy who courted Sarah, and after just a few months the two were going pretty regular. He was a porter for GWR and lived up toward St George. He would come for a drink at the Rising Sun after he was done working and they would walk home together. Now, it is not for me to pry into the relationship, and Sarah herself was always rather private about personal matters. But I don't think it is giving too much information to say the boy had a merry pair of lips and a fine physique from all the lifting of trunks on and off trains that he did on the railways. On those long walks home he would entertain her with all manner of laddish japes. Oh, you should have seen him leap, climb and lampoon from this thing to that! And should this boy have sung *you* one of his bawdy songs on a starlit Victorian evening then certainly you would have been as giddy about him as Sarah was. More than once on the way home, on an evening pleasant and warm, the two had fallen into some convenient shrubbery and taken the opportunity to share all manner of kisses: French kisses, little kisses, smooches, whispers, sweet-nothings, fervent entreaties, promises, fumblings, outpourings, tickles, snufflings, romantic declarations, doggerel and giggles. Now, while this sort of thing may be odious to the reader, to actually be involved in it is quite the most wonderful thing to be found across the whole, moonlit earth.

> *Don't you remember when,*
> *You lay beside me*
> *And you said you'd marry me,*
> *And not deny me.*
> *If I said I'd marry you,*
> *It was only for to try you,*
> *So bring your witness love,*
> *And I'll not deny you.*

Sarah had found the love that her spirit had called out for, and now that she was walking with that love she had the delicious, exhilarating feeling of being within destiny itself. It is a feeling at once like safety and like danger, and the closest thing to it is what the surfers down in Cornwall experience when they are inside a wave as it closes about them. The roaring and rushing is so overwhelming that there is nothing left but the purity of that moment. Sarah's heart was carried aloft on the love she had to give, and it went so high that she neglected to check whether this man could really be trusted, and whether or not her commitment was truly returned in kind. One day she received a letter from her beloved that informed her that he loved another and always had. Sarah had been a mere distraction, and that while he was sorry to have played with her emotions, he must now do the right thing and immediately cease to be her familiar.

Strange news is come to town,
Strange news is carried,
Strange news flies up and down,
That my love is married.
I wish them both much joy,
Though they can't hear me,
And may God reward him well,
For the slighting of me.

Now, Sarah received this letter at work, for her mother and father were of the type who see nothing untoward about opening letters addressed to their daughter, and indeed if there be any sign that a letter may have been sent by a young man with time on his hands and a pen in his pocket, then they would regard a thorough analysis of that letter as nothing short of a parental duty. For this reason, all love notes for Sarah were addressed to the Rising Sun, and she was accustomed to reading them furtively there as she worked, enjoying the champagne sensations one always feels on the reception of an amorous message. As soon as she read this one, however, which turned right about from all the previous, and marked the end of her love (indeed, it even retroactively destroyed what she had already experienced) the world juddered and spun round. She went outside and sat in the street. The letter hollowed out the cavity of her chest in one great brutal scoop, rather like someone deftly emptying a pumpkin of sludge and seed. In the aching space thus created, her heart began to tumble down and down. It quickly reached a kind of terminal velocity and she kept expecting it to crash into something and explode on impact. But such release never came. Sarah's poor heart fell headlong, tumbled through her belly, down into the cavernous earth, through the other side, across the sky, and through unending space. He was not who she thought he was. *She* was not who she thought *herself* to be. She was but a poor fool who could not tell love from emptiness, nor truth from equivocation. She could never love again. She saw a painful, dreary life spread before her, and clutching the letter in her fist she began to run. She ran first across the park that had been the runway of so many of their ardent take-offs. She speeded up. Her teeth clacked as she wheezed out great earthy sobs. She went over the bridge and over the lock. Then started up the hill into Clifton. She knew where she was headed. You too must have worked out where she was headed, dear reader, in a state like that and in a chapter like this. She was in despair and was going up to Clifton Suspension Bridge.

> *Oh, witness have I none,*
> *Save God Almighty,*
> *And may he reward you well,*
> *For the slighting of me.*
> *Her lips grew pale and wan,*
> *It made a poor heart tremble,*
> *To think she loved a one,*
> *Who proved deceitful.*

The hill is steep and, being a Victorian, Sarah Ann Henley's clothes were not particularly light. She had on all manner of shirts and blouses and bonnets and so forth, and also, being a rather fashionable young thing – with a handsome man to impress remember – she had beneath her skirts a crinoline: that ingenious series of hoops that women of the era used to puff out their dresses in an alluringly cake-like manner. Despite the weight of these stylistic commitments, Sarah gained speed rather than lost it as she assaulted the famous hill up to Clifton, which is almost as sheer in places as the rocky plunge of the gorge itself. She could not tell the difference between the tears and the sweat, nor did she mind them.

She ran straight out onto the bridge. It is hard to imagine that as she ran under the towers Sarah did not feel some dark twinge of bitter satisfaction that her final deed would form a more potent reply to the treacherous lover-boy than ever she could set to paper. And probably there would have been relief too: the relief of leaving her own supposed worthlessness and stupidity behind, and also the simple relief of having made it all the way to the top of such a gert hill and thus kinetically earning the coming descent. Whatever she felt, it was without so much as a qualm or a quiver that she leapt off the bridge and out into those dizzying acres of space that lie around it.

Now, I have tried to impress on all the good people of Bristol who have helped me with the present study the irrelevance of empirical truth to an urban legend. You see, an urban legend is a story that does well out in the wild chatland of our pubs and playgrounds; it is a story that – without Arts Council funding, a generous advance, or any artificial means whatsoever – *makes itself known*. Many folks have said to me: 'Oh, you won't want this one because it really happened…' or else, 'Shame this one aint true else you'd use it for sure!' To which I always reply, 'Forget what's true and what's not, and tell me the tale as it wants to be told!' That said, I do feel that it is important to relate to you, ladies and gentlemen of a sceptical era, that what I am about to relate seems to be eminently verifiable. It was seen directly by more than a handful of reliable witnesses, including a disgruntled and deeply cynical cabbie whose best interests dictated a flat-out denial of the whole affair. The aftermath was quickly dealt with by some very fastidious police officers who were on the scene almost immediately and the whole story was reported by both of our very reputable local newspapers.

Anyway, think what you like. The fact is, Sarah floated. The rushing air got up under that crinoline and held her aloft. It was like she was a puppet brandished by a giant, invisible hand. To those who watched astonished from Hotwells Road she appeared to stand motionless in the river of sky that runs silently through the gorge. What this felt like for her I can only guess. She would have been astonished presumably, probably too astonished to feel either disappointment or relief about the change of plan. I bet she made a few of those animalistic intakes of breath that people commonly make as they are falling off their bicycles. It was a cool, still evening, and no doubt she would have been able to hear the hammers still clanging softly down at the docks, and certainly gasps and astonished curses from Clifton Suspension Bridge. Apart from these ambient sounds there would have been the rhythmic whipping of her many skirts as the air splayed them open. Parachutes always have a hole in the top, and in order for Sarah to not tip over, a steady stream of air must have been rushing up past her legs, through her undergarments, over her belly and her spine, under her arms, up her neck, gently flicking past her ears, and finally playing with some strands of her dark hair as it took its leave and rejoined the ether.

Once in Victoria's golden age,
When crinolines were all the rage,
A dame in fashionable attire,
Would change her life for one up higher,
So up to Clifton Bridge she went,
And made a parachute descent.

The space that spans from the Avon up to the bridge must surely be Bristol's favourite chunk of emptiness – and it has never been so full of glory as it was that day! Sarah Ann Henley rang it like a bell. She drifted down and landed, with a considerably weighty and painful-sounding *thwack*, into that bank of cold, grey clay that accompanies the dirty river through the gorge.

There was a cabbie right there, and despite the entreaties of the good citizens who rescued the shaken Sarah from the muck, he point-blank refused to have her in his cab on account that he had just had it cleaned. Cabs in those days were rarely used by anyone except the well-healed. During the ensuing weeks of his notoriety, the selfish cabbie defended his decision to the last, arguing that it cannot be the cab driver's duty to rescue every waif and stray who happens to float down in front of him. One old gent I spoke to, a man well-versed in local lore, told me with confidence that it was actually the selfish cabbie himself who first suggested a special fund be set up to ferry common people to the hospital. And so it is that we have the selfish cabbie to thank for our ambulance service.

Sarah was carried up to the hospital on a stretcher in the end, and by the time she was placed on a ward she was famous. She was inundated with requests for interviews and, soon after, with proposals of marriage. These were sent by gentlemen moved by the pitiless deceit with which she had been formally treated, or who understood her as the beneficiary of a bona fide miracle, or who simply saw her square, pretty face staring out at them from the morning paper.

Sarah did not like to talk of what happened, for it marked an unhappy time in her life that she'd rather not revisit. Many years later, in 1901 I believe, she married a man called John who was kind, reliable and strong – and they both lived happily ever after.

THE CATACOMBS

REGARDING BRISTOL'S UNDERNEATH, there are some very interesting stories to be found, should one know where to look. Of course, you don't need to, because I have gone down and done the work for you. It is best to have a guide in these matters. Stories can be dangerous: some don't have much depth while others go down and down and down – so far down that it's impossible to reach the bottom. If you are thinking that it's always quite easy to reach the bottom of a story then I suggest that you go and talk to a journalist. Journalists have the unenviable task of turning deep and complex stories into stories so simple and shallow that we can eat them with a croissant. Journalists know well that to actually get to the bottom of some stories would involve not only undertaking a horrific multitude of teary-eyed interviews, but also a deeply unsettling re-evaluation of every single one of your most basic opinions, assumptions and life strategies. Stick with me, and I'll take you no deeper than is safe.

Mysterious Crimes #1

Say you found a dismembered foot or hand. Say you were a police officer and had no leads or really any idea where this appendage may have sprung from. Say forensic scientists and doctors could only tell you that it was from a healthy, living body, and that it had been severed by someone who knew what they were doing. Would you, in your capacity as an officer of the law, describe this phenomenon as 'suspicious'? Now, I'm an outsider to the profession, but I feel like this would pretty much fit the bill.

So you will be surprised to hear that Avon and Somerset Police decided that nothing was suspicious in no less than three separate cases of perfectly healthy hands or feet turning up without their owners. The good people at The History

Press have asked me to stay away from conspiracy theories. They want this book to be a light read. They want me to stick to the fun-day stuff. So, respecting their wishes, I'll move on for now. But I don't like it I tell you. I don't like it one bit.

An Entrance

Two of my informants, I'll call them Rachel and Jamie, lived on Park Street in the early 2000s, while they were students studying up the hill at the university. I was very keen to find people who lived around there, as I had heard some intriguing stories, all relating to a supposed network of tunnels that run beneath that part of town. For instance, there is the tale that the Dugout – a club that was central to the era of the Bristol Sound in the 1980s and '90s (featuring the Wildbunch, Massive Attack, Tricky, Portishead, et al.) – is accessible by tunnel, and that using these tunnels the luminaries of the scene still go down there and throw the odd secret reunion party. Many an old head has sworn to me that walking past the place of an evening (or an early morning) they've heard some sick beats leaking through the paving slabs. Street artist Banksy (real name Shauna Devere) is rumoured to know the tunnels well, and if you talk to traders up on the triangle they'll swear that, for the entire period preceding her takeover of Bristol Museum, she was seen going into Browns every morning and not emerging until closing time.

And yet, if there were a network of tunnels under Clifton, wouldn't they be a tourist attraction? Exeter is riddled with old Roman tunnels, and while no one knows why they were built, the council certainly knows how to stick a chap in a hard hat at the entrance and charge £7 a pop for a walk around in the dark. If there were tunnels in Bristol, surely someone would have monetised them. I'm pretty sure that underground is not magically exempt from the rapacious capitalist logic to which our society subscribes. Anyway, I wanted to get to the bottom of the story, which is why I was delighted to make the acquaintance of Rachel and Jamie.

These days the pair both live a long way from Park Street, and I met them in Jamie's tidy little flat in Willsbridge, just the other side of the river from Keynsham. Rachel answered the door. She was wearing a dress that made her look like an Andalucían flamenco dancer, though she is Somerset born and bred. She was cordial, but kept me at a distance, holding her head high and taking in my scruffy clothes and tatty notebook. I felt myself being analysed. It was like she was waiting for something to fall into place, like she wasn't quite ready to trust me. Jamie was not quite so sharp, but what he lacked in brains he made up for in brawn: the man was huge. His gargantuan shoulders sloped apologetically as he sat at the kitchen table over his tea. We began to talk. I could tell very quickly that Jamie was not good at withholding information. The light was coming through the window behind him and even his silhouette seemed to be saying more than he meant it to. It quickly became clear that whatever story they had to tell me made him morose and her wary. She lent against the kitchen cabinet, arms folded. She was cross with him for talking, I could feel it. I felt bad for coming into their lives like this, to force them to revisit what smelled like an unpleasant tale. But I was curious, and I knew my readers would be curious too. And so I began tracking the story in the usual way, although as you will see I did not get very far on this occasion. As the clock overlooking the neat little kitchen ticked, I felt like I was moving deeper into the pair's relationship, crowded by Jamie's hulking form and Rachel's formidable intellect. Eventually something happened and I felt I had to turn back. Perhaps someone with greater dedication to the truth would have gone on. I apologise, reader, but on this occasion the story seemed just too dangerous for me to follow to the end.

In their student days, during the early 2000s, Jamie and Rachel lived with a fluctuating band of ten to twenty people. They ran a rollicking co-op house, where all the normal pranks and snogs took place. The house was a rickety nine-bedroom place on Park Street. They would have grand dinners where instant noodles would be served from huge steaming tureens. An aperitif of White Lightning cider would be followed by Cup-a-Soup for starters. Platters stacked with microwaved burgers and Turkey Twizzlers were passed around with great flamboyance, and cheap blue wine – served with a dash of cola – was quaffed and savoured as the evening wore on. Naturally, everyone present would be as naked as the day they were born, minus the odd bow tie or cowboy hat. It was on just such an evening that the discovery was made.

I've often thought that those pursuits that are seen as the sole preserve of adult life, debauched soirees such as I'm currently intimating for instance, are actually ways in which grown-ups can rediscover the joys of childhood. To this end, Rachel and Jamie and their crew liked to play the odd game of hide and seek. On the evening in question their housemate Beauty had decided to hide in the cupboard under the stairs. Beauty was very competitive and for this reason she had climbed over the Hoover and shuffled various bits of detritus so that she would not be visible if the door was opened. Leaning against the back wall of the cupboard she felt something pressing into her. It was a handle. Without thinking, she reached back and twisted it. Luckily, Beauty's grip on life was tenacious and she prevented herself tumbling into the void. She could feel stone steps going down. They were smooth and damp. It was cold. There was a slight breeze coming up the stairs. She screamed for the others to come quick, unable to take her eyes off the darkness before her.

It was a basement, of course. The landlord had never mentioned a basement. Everyone went down there in a state of high excitement. I asked Rachel if she had had that feeling like no one had been there in a long time, which I myself know well from exploring abandoned buildings and so forth looking for ghosts. Rachel just looked at me, trying to ascertain how much I knew. I think that she thought I knew more than I actually did know. I tried to ignore her mistrust and kept the questions flowing, staying naïve and cheerful. There were stacks of dusty boxes down in the basement. It is not remembered what was in them. There were several large rooms. The floor was compacted stony dirt. Each member of the party poked around on their own. A few had mobiles and lit the way using the dim light from their screens, the others used lighters. Only Rachel had a torch. They were already planning the parties they were going to have down there. It was going to be epic. Then Jamie discovered it. It was right at the back, behind a pile of pallets and crates. He looked guilty as he described it to me, his head lolling slightly on his thick neck, his gaze fixed on the baby blue tablecloth in front of him.

Rachel and Jamie are not a couple but they have stayed close to one another since their uni days, both emotionally and geographically. As Jamie is talking, Rachel tenses up like a rope with someone on the end of it. But she does not stop him.

'There was like a patch that was, like, darker. It was just this sort of sheet. It was like a bed sheet but it was black. I touched it and there was nothing behind it. I said, "Guys...," you know, so the guys would come over. And I pulled it back and even though you couldn't see anything you knew there was nothing there. It was an entrance. I mean like, the entrance to the tunnel.'

The party stood at the mouth of the passage. It was rough and a little crumbly but seemed solid enough. They could feel a steady breeze coming from it. There was some discussion about what to do next. Some of them were overawed.

Rachel wanted them to leave it well alone. But most were still in a mood for fun and adventure, or they were overpowered by curiosity.

'People wanted to see what was down there. I didn't want to see. Like… I didn't need to see. I thought we should go back,' said Jamie.

'Why did you lead us down there then?' interjected Rachel.

'Because everyone told me to!' said Jamie, a maddened, childish tone sneaking into his voice.

'And you have to do what people tell you?' Rachel retorted, but still looked at him to continue, as if it were now inevitable that the story be told in full.

'I took the torch and we started going down. It was very dark. If you pointed the torch straight ahead the beam just like disappeared.'

'How big was it?' I asked.

'It was pretty wide. You could walk along next to someone. But it wasn't tall enough to stand.'

'I could stand,' Rachel contradicted. 'Most of us could.' I looked at huge Jamie. He wasn't built for underground tunnels.

'It went straight. It was headed up the street [Park Street] but it was sloping a little bit down.'

'It was going steeply down,' Rachel said, turning her head away and staring hard at the kettle.

'Why was it sloping down though?' Jamie asked. I waited, not quite sure if this was a rhetorical question. When he said nothing I replied, 'I'm not sure.'

'We went down and down. At first everyone was laughing. But after a couple of minutes everyone went quiet. I don't know why but everyone was whispering. At one part water was coming out of this little hole and was running down in a channel in the side of the passage. Then later we found out that this used to be like this spring that everyone used to drink from, but then it got blocked off because they wanted people to, like, pay for water.' I later researched this story about the spring and duly found out about St John's Conduit, a life-giving stream that once ran down the length of Park Street, and which indeed is rumoured to have been redirected underground by a prominent Bristol water company. Jamie continued: 'Everyone stopped talking and you could just hear the water running. I was at the front. It was scary. It's funny because I've always been kind of scared of the dark but I just like ignore it. I don't like not knowing, you know? Neither does she.' He motioned at Rachel, who said nothing but seemed to soften a little. 'But I thought to myself "I'll keep going until someone says we should turn back."'

'But we were just following you!' Rachel's voice cracked slightly, no longer sounding stern, just regretful. 'We all thought everyone else wanted to go on, but none of us actually did. Someone could have said something...'

Jamie's brow was furrowed. His knuckles were white. They were both silent for a long time. And very still. It was like being in a painting. I had the feeling I could get up and leave and neither of them would move a millimetre. Eventually I asked, 'So what was down there?'

For what seemed a long time no one moved. Then I noticed that Jamie's shoulders had started to judder. The movement became more and more intense until it was like he was operating one of those drills workmen use to break up the road. He made a sound, or maybe it was an attempt at words. It sounded like perhaps he said, 'There was...' But a moment after these syllables left his mouth the mug that he held in his right hand cracked and caved in on itself. Hot tea sploshed all over his vest. His hand was bleeding. Rachel rushed over. They were both crying. I was stunned. He had just crushed an 'I <3 Bristol' mug with one hand. Rachel was shouting at me, 'Just get out!' I obeyed without really knowing what I was doing and emerged into the street in a daze.

Theories of the Catacombs

What do you think is down in the tunnels? Who built them? Why? When? The people of Bristol have given me various answers to these questions. A popular one is that they were used to transport slaves across the city. Some hold that this was to keep the enslaved hidden from polite society, who had no desire to see the hideous anguish upon which their beautiful townhouses had been built. Others claim that the slaves had to be transported in secret to keep angry crowds of anti-slavery campaigners from attacking the traders and trying to free their human cargo.

Certainly some of the tunnels were connected to the mining industry. For hundreds of years pretty much everyone in Hanham and Kingswood was a miner. Their mines were not run by companies or the state but by the miners themselves. Those folk were a fierce lot, living underground themselves much of the time, or else in treehouses and benders in the woods. They spoke a harsh dialect that was forbidden to outsiders (there are rumours that some of the older people up in Kingswood still speak it). There are even better rumours that communities of people still live down in the mines. Cavers have reported seeing, through a narrow crack or down a dangerous shaft, a flickering light. Floating with it on the stale air will come the sound of a foreign tongue being spoken. They tell me it sounds like the Bristol accent gone feral, turned loose from English altogether: nothing left but undulating vowels and buzzing zeds.

Further towards town, it is said that if you failed to pay your tab in the Fire Engine pub in St George, the landlady Bridey Stamp would send you down to the basement where there was an entrance to the mines. There you would labour until you could bring up what you owed in coal.

Others have told me that the tunnels were all about smuggling contraband. There were apparently places where you could sail a brig directly into the catacombs to unload your duty-free treats, although how they hid the entrances I do not know. Where the goods were unloaded is more obvious: the vast majority of pubs near the docks are connected to the catacombs. Pirates found this handy both for moving ill-gotten goods around the city and for escape routes. Who knows if it was stupidity or overconfidence that led them to bestow names like The Hole in the Wall to the best-connected establishments?

Likewise, it is said that to this very day the catacombs are still used to deliver illegal drugs hither and thither across the city. An underground delivery service that is literally underground. I've been told about baggies full of sparkling white powder handed up through drains and lunchboxes stuffed with stinky weed appearing from under manhole covers.

I've heard from many that the Portway Tunnels along the gorge were used for shelter during the Blitz, and I wouldn't be surprised if most Bristolians found some way down into the safety of the catacombs during the long nights of bombing. Considering the capacity and reach of the network of tunnels it is a wonder that the Luftwaffe were able to take a single life.

On the rocky sides of the gorge and peppered through the scrubland of Clifton Downs you'll find many caves. I was told there were homeless people living in these caves, but when I crawled into the entrance to one of them and had a look around I was reluctant to categorise the inhabitants as 'homeless'. There was a lovely living space furnished with a very tasteful three piece from John Lewis. A table in the corner showed the remains of a breakfast of porridge and fruit. I chewed on a handful of goji berries and kept exploring. I had to scramble up a wall and make it through another little entrance to get to the bedrooms. There was one that was exceedingly large: the light from my phone getting lost in the expanse, here and there picking out a picture frame or a vase. The next room I tried was very pokey and rather claustrophobic; besides, the bed was for a child. The last one was just right I'd say. Nice and cosy. The bed looked very inviting: with brushed cotton sheets and an eiderdown bedspread. I'll just have a little lie down, thought I.

There is a video online which shows some people from the council going down underneath one of the towers of the suspension bridge. They are investigating rumours that there was something built down there, and what they find is more incredible than they ever could have imagined. There is a huge cavern, presumably hollowed out from the rock of the gorge, and then several tunnels shooting off in different directions. It shows signs of all being built at the same time as the bridge but there is no structural reason for it to exist. The staff present, who are all engineers and professionals, and whose knowledge of Bristol is unequalled, are stunned.

People spend an awful lot of time staring up at the stars, waxing lyrical about how little we know and what might be up there, but they rarely reflect on what is going on underneath their feet.

The Secret Life-Giving Fountain of Eternal Youth and the Dirty Hippies

There is a story that before Brunel and the boys built the railway along the Avon, there used to be hot springs in the side of the gorge, where the good people of Bristol would go to bathe. It was these springs that gave Hotwells its name. The water was rich with minerals and very good for the health, and for years and years Bristolians were uncommonly vigorous. Apparently, those who went to these springs regularly were living to truly biblical ages: well over 200 years in many cases, although this was kept hush hush lest some top-hatted realist recognise the springs as a source of profit. The people sensed that the place could not be kept magical and be turned over to commerce. To finish an honest day's work with a splash around with your fellow townsfolk, to listen to the adults gossip and the children play, to lie back in water that has been warmed in the womb of Mother Earth herself and watch an old grandpa and his little granddaughter fishing together on the banks of the muddy old Avon… Well, if that's not the secret to long life then I don't know what is. That's how we should be living my friends! But when industrialisation came and Brunel wanted to build his Great Western Railway it was decided that connecting Bristol to Ham Green and Pill trumped the people's constitutional, and so the hot springs were filled in with grit and the railway was built right over them.

Now, it seems to me that the presence of the hot springs can explain the curious reaction of the authorities to the parties that took place along the same bank of the Avon. These gatherings were legendary, especially among certain hippies of Bristol. I'm talking about a particular branch of hippy subculture that I should take a moment to distinguish: the *dirty* hippies. These are not to be confused with the rich ones who run superfood companies and have hot tubs. These dirty hippies had bugger all but a good time, and this story actually concerns how they almost take a bath but then don't. Anyway, to understand you have to know those curious natural amphitheatres that line the gorge. You access them by a series of archways that go under the railway. Network Rail or somebody has made an attempt to block them off from the public by putting gates in these archways and keeping them locked. But the public exerts a more immense pressure than almost anyone suspects. We push relentlessly inward on everything, and even the tiniest fissure will soon grow to a crack, and once there is a crack the game is up, for soon it will split and the public will come rushing in. And that is exactly what has happened down in the rocky arenas that line the gorge. Whoever is official custodian of the land down there was never going to be able to block them off forever, for the entire area is absolutely riddled with entrances into the catacombs.

The acoustics in these amphitheatres is quite magical, and if I was standing at one end and you at the other I could tell you one of my fabulous stories at a whisper. This was a great boon when it came to throwing parties: the sound of the beats and the bass and the hook ringing out across the space was bewitching. Unfailingly, the plod would come to stomp out the fun at some point. It must have been very frustrating for them though, for the gorge is a tremendous playground for sound, and the music would be reflecting and refracting and diffracting about like nobody's business – leaving them hard-pressed to tell where it was actually originating. More often than not they would smash through one of the locked gates, convinced they had found the party, only to find a space empty of human life. They would look around, dwarfed by the sheer sides of rock shooting up all around them. Little whispering saplings growing from the crevices, ivy draping from mossy ledges, and little waterfalls trickling down from Leigh Woods high above.

If the police ever did get close to the actual party, the dirty hippies always had their sound system in various carts and barrows, and they would simply wheel the whole party down into the tunnels and pop up in a different part of the gorge to start again. You have to pity the authorities, really, to be always dealing with the haunting miscreance of the people. It can't be easy.

It is strange though that the police were under order to raid these gorge parties in the first place, because there isn't a soul to disturb down there (apart from Goram and Vincent that is, but they sleep very deeply). The dirty hippies themselves tend to claim that it was all part of a sinister conspiracy plotted by the highest echelons of the establishment, the aim being to keep the people of Bristol down-hearted and in their place. If such conspirators exist, I suspect that they were concerned about dowsing. Dowsing is an old technique for finding water beneath the ground using two rods held lightly in the hands. And seeing as people at these parties can get very thirsty, and that hippies have a liking for ancient technologies, it is very possible that one of the partygoers would indeed start dowsing. If this should have happened then the dowser would have been very likely to locate the hot springs. The dowsing rods would have been going wacko, and the hippies would have got themselves into a state of great excitement. You can bet your biggest joss stick that the whole party would have been mobilised to rip up the tracks and dig down until the hot springs bubbled up from the womb of the world once more. Rail connectivity would be sacrificed for the happiness and wellbeing that had once been the Bristolian's birthright. And the powers that be couldn't have that. Not on their watch.

The Dark Street

Residents of St George, Lawrence Hill and Redfield would not be best pleased if I did not include for them the incredible story about Church Road. You've heard of the 'dark web' right? It's a hidden version of the Internet that us ordinary folk use. You may know too about the fairies before Disney got to them, when they lived in an alternate 'dark' version of our world, with every house, every church, every tavern up here having a twisted version that was located exactly underneath it in the fairy kingdom.

Now, do you know where the big Lidl is in Lawrence Hill? Well, it is said that directly underneath that bit of Church Road is a dark, ghostly version of the street, with shops and street lamps and postboxes and everything else. Naturally, there are conflicting reports. Some say that everything is eerily similar to what you find topside, like it's a kind of back-up Church Road. Others claim that it was a functioning street in Victorian times, but then had to be buried for tax reasons. In this version, all the shops are preserved exactly as they were, with everything still on the shelves. Much of the produce is past its best, of course, but it's said that the bonbons in the sweetshop are still edible. A man told me up in St George, in the old Italian barbers opposite the park there (which itself is something of a preserve of years gone by), that it is not at all haunted and that his daughter takes her kids down there on a rainy Saturday for a delightful outing back in time.

Mysterious Crimes #2

By far the most disturbing tale of the underground tunnels came my way in Broadmead one day. I had set up a stall in the street with a big sign saying '*Come Tell Me Your Bristol Urban Legends!*' One lady, Cathy Eldritch, had a lot to say about the underground tunnels. Now I'm afraid to say that at first I had Cathy labelled as something of a crackpot. However, her account did have a certain logic to it, and it connected with much else that I have found out. For long stretches her monologue would descend into unusable rubbish, but then suddenly she would be talking about a familiar Bristol tale and I would think 'This is it!' Then we would plunge back down into murky conspiracist fantasies until, once more, we would pop up in the middle of another classic Bristol mystery. In this manner she suggested to me the hidden connections between many well-known legends. Now, much of what she said would put me at risk of some hefty litigation from some big trousers in town and the last thing I want is to be sued by a prominent organisation for implicating them in a death cult.

I can, however, recount to you my own sanitised version of what Cathy told me regarding human sacrifice in Bristol. According to her, the catacombs were built in Pagan times and were used in a rite where a young prince or princess was sacrificed. The ceremony is shrouded in mystery but the idea seemed to be that the royal teen was given to the earth in order that their pure hearts would become deposits of gold. Apparently, the trick rarely worked for the priests could never resist having their wicked way with the young royals, and this act of defilement disrupted the magic. In Roman times the catacombs were given over to the cult of Mithras, a mystery religion that was popular with the powerful Roman elite all over the empire. Without a single exception the worship of Mithras took place underground and to this date no one knows what the devotees did down there or what they believed. Cathy assured me that it was not likely to be pretty, for underground is where one finds the basest energies, and any religion that takes place underground will sure as hellfire be devoted to the most base among human purposes.

There is a certain spot, directly beneath the cathedral, where the Roman authorities used to execute early Christians. They would do this by throwing the offenders down a long shaft: the bottom of which no one has ever fathomed. Their screaming would be heard for a long time, and you might fancy that it was gone until, after ten or so long seconds of silence, another little auditory fragment of the martyr's pain would come bubbling up from the darkness.

These days the catacombs are the main place of worship for Bristol's most powerful Satanists. Their rituals often start in a regular church, ideally the cathedral itself, for such places are particularly powerful venues when it comes to magical rites. With minimal preparation – as little as placing a few symbols (innocuous enough to lay persons) – at key points around the sanctuary, holy spaces can be manipulated until they actually *reverse positive energy waveforms*. That means anyone present who is full of a bounteous love of humankind, or has a touching empathy for the plight of animals, is unwittingly aiding the twisted purposes of the Satanic priesthood. Of course, these services never advertise their Satanic affiliation to the general public; ostensibly they are special functions of one kind or another: award ceremonies, commemorative events and so forth.

Frequently there will be a sacrificial victim present in the church. Now, not much of the detail here is repeatable, but I will relay some general things. The Satanic cult manages these offerings in a few different ways, depending on who's available. Sometimes the sacrifice knows the role they are to play but are too drugged or brainwashed or terrified to speak out. Preferably, however, they remain blissfully unaware of their fate until the last possible moment. They sit through a flute recital, smiling the whole way. And the smile only broadens as they are called up to the stage. Their parents or carers give them an encouraging thumbs-up, but they are in on the conspiracy and have sold the poor child into the ceremony out of greed and devotion (which amount to the same thing for Satanists). When the average 16-year-old is given a bravery award they are unlikely to turn from the stage and run just because they suddenly notice a floral wreath in the shape of the pentagram. You don't refuse an award on the grounds that someone has a sinister goatee, or because a little knot of people near the stage are chanting something in a whisper as you go past. No, you walk up on to the stage and accept the certificate, trying to ignore the devouring eyes of the dignitary who is presenting it to you. You do your best not to wince as his handshake squeezes like a threat. You are asked to stand by the side of the stage, out of view of the rest of the crowd. You are standing on tiptoe, trying to catch a glimpse of your aunt, when someone comes and taps you on the shoulder.

When the regular people are coming out of the church thinking that the ceremony is over it is in fact only just beginning. An exclusive party has moved downstairs into the crypt, and from there into the catacombs of Bristol. The despicable things that go on down there make the sacrifices of yesteryear seem humane. The more anguish the young victims experience, Ms Eldritch informed me, the more effectively the religious aims of the Satanists are fulfilled.

Cathy told me about one rite that particularly caught my interest. In a regular church or temple the routine is to pray for other people to have a kind of vague wellbeing. Conversely, the idea behind attending the Church of Satan is to obtain a specific goal relating to your own self-interest. It is an appealing prospect, as well as being more realistically achievable, and this accounts for its popularity among the elite, who like to think of themselves as no-nonsense pragmatists. This particular ceremony must be officiated by a Bishop of Satan and is always sponsored by a devotee who is looking to gain a specific place of power and influence. The meaning of the ritualistic actions involved (and I understand the ceremony takes over 24 hours to complete) have to do with mastery and control. Along with various ritual implements – blades, scrolls, horns, chalices and so forth – a healthy human adult is needed. The latter's role is very simple: first a hand is removed, and then a foot. This can actually be done with modern surgical implements, so you don't have to do any of that dreadfully inconvenient messing around with impractical silver daggers and copper sickles that are fiddly to sharpen. Once you have the hands and the feet the adult can be disposed of. They are, of course, thrown down the hole that lies beneath the cathedral to join the martyrs of old.

The hand, which symbolises control, and the foot, which symbolises determination, then go through many more layers of rites, which I will not repeat here for fear that someone should try them at home. The final segment of the liturgy involves the appendages being placed into a certain underground stream that runs beneath Bristol. This stream meanders along happily underneath us and eventually emerges back up into the light in a nondescript ditch somewhere in the hinterlands of the city (*see* Mysterious Crimes #1).

Cathy Eldritch may well be a crackpot. But perhaps it takes a crackpot to see what is going on under this town. No other explanation of the appearance of severed appendages cuts it. They came from somewhere, didn't they? You're not stupid: you know the powerful make their backroom deals and receive their golden handshakes. Do you really think they would turn up their noses at the ultimate deal, with Satan himself? And if you were Satan, would it not be in your interests to stipulate that the hopeful should commit some horrific act? For that way they are more likely to be yours forever: having gone down that far it would take a miracle for them to find the light again. Besides, they will have power, wealth and influence as a consolation for the loss of their goodness and humanity.

It all makes for a sickening story, but not such a surprising one. People go missing. Everything plays into the hands of a few wealthy individuals. Beneath the veneer of respectable public personas lies a machinery that is hidden from view. Severed hands and feet wash up from drains, and the authorities refuse to investigate. What is going on? Of all the people I have spoken to in this city, only Cathy Eldritch has been brave enough to grab the issue by the horns.

THE HOMELESS WANDERER AND OTHER STORIES

TO **WHAT NEW** lows has humanity sunk in the week you are reading this? Stories such as I tell tend to have a nice shape, with some rocky times for the characters involved, but then everything resolving and ending well as they meet their happily ever afters. It is very satisfying telling stories: like wrapping up a present. You take a manageable wadge of humanity, fold the colourful paper all around it, and finish it off with a little bow. But in the darker moments it sometimes seems to me that the human story actually takes an unpackageable downward plunge: an agonising descent into vengeance, violence and hypocrisy. My mum went to school at the Pro-Cathedral in Clifton and the nuns there used to tell the students to ask three questions of everything they said: Is it true? Is it kind? Is it useful? I'm sure the above impression would receive a negative on one or other of these criteria, so pay it no mind. I mention it only because it is how I felt when I heard about the gang who had taken to beating up homeless people for sport.

Of course, the homeless themselves knew about them before anybody else, for word travels fast on the streets. A violent criminal element was stalking those who slept rough, and I'm afraid to say that the people of Bristol either did not notice or did not care. But great tribulation can sometimes bring forth great heroism, and the story goes that a homeless vigilante arose to protect others who found themselves on the streets each night. This mysterious person would prowl the shadows on the lookout for the gang. Never attacking first, she or he would wait until they caught the villains in the act: encircling their victim as they slept in a doorway or upon a bench. Only then would the hero strike, moving so quickly that the gang didn't know what hit them. Not trusting the law to dole out fitting punishment, the Homeless Wanderer (I thought of this name) would enrol the offenders in a course of what you might call *physical re-education*. Whatever this entailed, it worked, because the attacks on homeless folk soon stopped.

I've heard this story several times from people who are or who have been homeless in Bristol. Make of it what you will. I don't want to bring it into the little vignettes that I am about to share, which are just some of the stories about people who have lived life on the streets in our town. But I do invite you to ponder as you meet the characters I am going to introduce you to, is *this* the Homeless Wanderer?

The King of the Tramps

Many years ago, there was an old fella whom folks on the street called the 'King of the Tramps'. He was famously garrulous and would walk around singing various songs of his own invention. Having once been a bank manager he was still fond of giving orders to his underlings, who, fortunately for them, were now all imaginary. He was rather fond of a can of cider or seventeen and had previously been into other dangerous substances. He had a song that detailed his history in regards to such matters. It went:

> *In the '60s I took cannabis,*
> *In the '70s I took heroin,*
> *In the '80s sweet cocaine,*
> *But in the '90s cider, cider, cider,*
> *I said cider, cider, cider, cider, cider.*

You would be right to assume that I am a general supporter of urban legends, but that doesn't mean that I think that they're all benign. Stories are the means by which we apprehend the world, and the one about the homeless predominantly finding themselves on the streets because of addiction is a misapprehension. The statistics clearly show that the biggest causes of homelessness are structural factors like tenancy rights and rising rent prices, factors that affect people whatever their narcotic predilections. For this reason, a story of a bank manager who drugs himself alone does play into a rather pernicious and unhelpful story about what causes homelessness. That said, he was who he was, and I've always admired those who live by the maxim: *whatever you are doing, do it properly*. It was in recognition of the gusto with which this character committed himself to inebriation that Bristol hallowed him with the title the 'King of the Tramps'.

The Big Issue

There was a man who was homeless for many years and who was famous for his clean living, never touching drugs and only having a tipple at festive occasions. I include him here because of a remarkable story I heard. I'll call him Mr J. Being an enterprising chap, Mr J. got a gig selling *The Big Issue* and was slowly working his way toward getting back into permanent accommodation and something like a normal life. This is, I hope you appreciate, a formidably hard task. I think that really most people would have little hope of accomplishing it, should they ever be unlucky enough to have to try. If anyone could do it though it was Mr J. He worked hard selling magazines up in Clifton. And then something incredible happened. Mr J. often used to stand right outside Bristol Museum to sell his wares, and naturally he was a bit miffed when it unexpectedly closed down for a refurbishment. However, imagine his delight when the place reopened a few weeks later and Mr J. saw that Banksy had done his takeover. Banksy being as popular as he is, there were queues right down the street all day every day for months. The line was 100 yards long minimum, and at least five people deep the whole way. It crawled along. Most people weren't sensible enough to bring something to while away the time, but luckily Mr J. was there to furnish them with a little reading matter. It was a captive market and he did a roaring trade. The best part is that that actually Mr J. knows Banksy to look at him, and knows him by his real name, Hewlett Packard. Mr J. had seen Hewlett every morning for the whole time the museum was closed going into Browns. If Hewlett caught J.'s eye, he would wink, which is how he had known the artist was working on something special.

They say the exhibition saved the museum from bankruptcy; well it also made Mr J. so much money that he was able not only to get a house, but also to get one on the beach. He had always wanted to retire back to the place where he came from first: Jamaica. You bet your bottom dollar he's sitting on his porch now, listening to the sea wash the shoreline. England hadn't always treated him well, but every year he sends a Christmas card back over to Bristol, thanking his friend Mr Hewlett Packard.

Mr Tomato Man

There was a man who lived homeless up in Clifton, not too far from the triangle where Mr J. worked. However, this was a fair few years ago they say: in the early 1980s when I was but a babber. He was rumoured to be a professor from the university. He had been discredited. Perhaps he faked some results. Perhaps he was framed. Perhaps he had discovered something that powerful forces in Bristol would rather stay hidden. Whatever it was, this man had been ejected from the ivory tower and had fallen on hard times. He could not afford to keep paying the bills and the rent. His boyfriend left him. Life on the streets is gruelling, and the prof tried to stay focused on the simple pleasures. He liked to stroll around the buildings of the university, still having a lot of love for the old place. He was partial to tomato sandwiches, and there was a girl who worked in a sandwich shop up there who knew this and would make him up a few at the end of the day. He would sit there on the steps to Browns and enjoy them, watching the sunset resting on the sandy buildings and slowly turn them as red as the tomatoes in his sarnies. Many people knew him. He was a quiet man, and a benign presence with a smile for everybody. The story goes that when he died, in a cold snap early one April, those who knew him were amazed to see a little tomato plant growing right in the spot where he used to sit. It grew to be a big healthy thing that made your hands sticky if you touched it and that you could smell from halfway up Park Street. That summer, there were tomatoes enough for everybody.

Bear the Poet

A homeless person who is sorely missed is Bear the poet. Bear used to make a bit of coin busking his poetry. For £1 you could get one from the impressive collection that he kept stored in his head. They say he had memorised over 1,000 poems. They were all strange and funny and wise. For £2 he would improvise a poem for you. All you needed to do was give him three words, or else tell him a little bit about yourself, and he could make one up on the spot. Bear's poems would lead you a merry dance, with sundry stories and jokes caught in there like driftwood, and the whole lot bouncing along and never missing a beat.

Bear was well-loved on the streets, not to mention at various venues about town. You'd see him performing on the stage at the Fleece one night and sat on Turbo Island with a tin the next. The way he died is very tragic, for he was beaten up in a random attack. His funeral was well attended by people from all walks of life. Bear had touched many with his spirit and his poetry.

The police said that there was no chance of bringing his attackers to justice. I find myself hoping that the Homeless Wanderer did not give up quite so easily.

THE DREADED HUMMADRUZ

THIS IS A tale of a furious seeking for something that's everywhere. It has something of the religious about it. You'll find that the seekers are fixed on their quest with a cultic enthusiasm. They go on about a 'Source'. They confidently predict a 'Final Revelation'; strange theories abound, and each devotee clamours to outdo the last in the brutal extremities of their commitment to the faith.

Among the disbelievers, on the other hand, you are bound to encounter that attribute always found among those loyal to mainstream opinion: an obstinate and reactionary grip on the explainable. This last group is the larger, of course, and it is also the more fanatical – although much less aware of its own fanaticism. They are duty-bound to ignore the unexplained, and their unreflective faith in the conventional story of 'what exists and what does not' gives them really quite fantastical powers to simply not perceive phenomena that happens to jeopardise this story.

There are two categories of believer. The first are those you might expect: researchers of paranormal activity and the like. Books about UFOs and Secrets-of-the-Pyramids jostle on their shelves. The reason this group thinks, for example, that the moon landings are fake (or that the moon is hollow and full of Nazis, or is covered in secret invisible structures etc., etc.) is not because they feel they have discovered a solid truth in the way that a scientist does. It is rather that they have discovered a way to *reclaim* some truth *back* from scientific solidity. They are, in fact, the exact opposite of scientists, for instead of meticulously adding stuff to the empirical story of everything, they find ways to carefully push stuff out of it. And who can blame them? Consider the moon for instance. It is a very cruel demotion that science has inflicted on our satellite: downgraded to mere rock after all those delightful ages spent being cheese! Anyway, treat of them how you will, you know the type: you'll find them on the Internet, happily constructing a sprawling metropolis of Speculation and Counter-Claim, unobstructed by the puritanical sanity of the majority.

The second category of believers are the unlucky ones. For them the unexplained is not a hobby; rather it is a most unwelcome and painful intrusion into their lives. I am speaking of those wretched few who find that they *cannot escape the unexplained*. While the denizens of normalcy and the conspiracy theorists gather at the opposite sides of the party, who is left in the middle, naked and alone? On one side there is the wrought-iron Ordinariness of the norms, which refuses to recognise their plight. On the other there is a group who, while they do admit the existence of certain occult horrors, are only interested in the victims' pain so far as it can be woven into their dark tapestry of deliberately preposterous conspiracy theories. Unlike everyone else, those who are genuinely threatened by the paranormal in this way really *need* the paranormal to be rationally explained. In some cases, their very lives depend upon it.

This story concerns a noise, a noise that only some people can hear. Enough people that we are talking about it here, but not enough for it to be accepted into the official list of existing things. It is a noise that drives people to madness. It is a noise that alienates people from their communities. It is a plague. No one knows where it comes from, or if it really exists. It is the Bristol mystery that eventually brought curious investigators flocking from all over the world. They call it the *Hummadruz*.

* * *

Lou Arthur moved from London to Westbury-on-Trym on the outskirts of Bristol to take a job working in the university in 1979. One night she was lying in her bed when she started to hear a kind of low buzzing or rumbling noise. She assumed

that it was a lorry idling outside. Only it was getting steadily louder. It quickly became apparent that it was not coming
from the road. Ms Arthur's next thought was that it was an
aeroplane. Probably on its way to the airport on the other side
of the city, or else a test flight from Filton Aerodrome. She
tried to go back to sleep. However, now the sound had pla-
teaued and was not getting louder or quieter as a plane would
as it soared overhead. She pulled herself out of bed and looked
out the window. She could see the street glowing innocu-
ously in the lamplight and, beyond that, the thick darkness of
the woods. She could see the rugged outline of the treetops
against the clouded sky. What she could not see was any likely
source for the sound. Lou tried once more to go back to sleep
but found it impossible. Eventually she pulled an overcoat
round her pyjamas and went out into the street.

The quality of the hum changed only slightly when Lou
got outside. She walked up the street both ways and it kept
the same pitch and volume wherever she was. She got in her
Hillman Minx and started it up, relieved when the throaty
engine obliterated all other sound. She drove around, searching for a source, but every time she stopped and turned off
the engine it still seemed to be coming from everywhere.
A few hours went by and she tried to establish its periphery.
She pictured it like a cloud, squatting on the land. It seemed
to stop at the river, and when she crossed over the suspension
bridge and listened in Leigh Woods she heard only the gentle
sound of the leaves and the slow creak of trees. The other way,
out past Filton to Stoke Gifford and beyond, she could not
find its end.

To come in on your first day of a new job raving about
a sound that only you can hear is not something you find
suggested in *How to Win Friends and Influence People*, and a
combination of this poor introduction and her increasing
sleeplessness meant that Lou found herself quickly ostracised

by her colleagues at the university. These days it is fairly routine to be sacked, or so it seems to me. The previous generation's experience was different, however. The unions were strong and, by and large, folks stayed in their jobs for life. In place of sacking though, the baby-boomers had developed a sort of witch-hunt that never climaxed in anything. Lou Arthur became a pariah, and her colleagues routinely traced all mistakes back to her. And it was indeed true that the poor woman's work was not what it could be, and this was because the entirety of her considerable energy was channeled into finding the source of the hum. She lived for the night, merely surviving the day.

The most common thing people would tell Lou would be that she was suffering from tinnitus. Lou became increasingly strained at this assertion. She would impatiently explain that it couldn't be tinnitus because the noise could not be heard when she put her hands over her ears. The theory that people usually suggested after tinnitus was even harder for Lou to countenance. They would say something like, 'Well, I've always had good hearing,' or else, more blatantly, 'Perhaps it's like those voices people hear?' The angry denials of madness that proceeded from Lou at this stage did nothing to repair people's trust in her sanity. It was thus that the tension between Lou and the rest of society was ratcheted up, each conversation pushing her a bit closer to total alienation.

* * *

The psychiatric profession, who are normality's frontline troops, insist that the hummadruz is a psychosomatic symptom of some kind. 'These people will sometimes not hear the noise when they're away from home and you'll often find that they're living in a home environment that's gone badly wrong. They scan their environment for the cause of their distress and latch on to this noise.' So a certain Dr Hazell told the *Independent* in June 1994 after an outbreak of the hummadruz. The cure, said he, is for the sufferer to reinterpret the noise as non-harmful and so reduce their awareness of it. Simple as that. You can almost hear Lou Arthur's anger pouring down the decades like boiling hot tar. The good doctor went on: 'It's like appearances of the Virgin Mary, isn't it? It's very much a question of belief.'

∗ ∗ ∗

Lou met Andrea in the car park of the university. She had just had a particularly disastrous meeting. She had genuinely gone in there with the intention of not mentioning the mysterious hum that pervaded her life but found herself unable to avoid the topic. The hummadruz was like a breezeblock on the trampoline of every conversation she had, and all her marbles rolled inexorably toward it. Sometimes she dreamed about it getting louder and louder until finally she was absorbed entirely. It was a relief. She imagined this was what it would be like to find the source. Lou wouldn't mind if the hummadruz obliterated the world, it was the coexistence of the two that she couldn't bear. Anyway, she was stood in the car park with her head in her hands. Unfortunately for her, Lou was one of those people who just *has* to know the truth. She doesn't want to know *her* truth, or *a* truth, she doesn't want wisdom, or ancient secrets, or the truth behind the truth, she doesn't want to uncover the ultimate reality or to know that everything is really an infinite web of fluctuating energy, she doesn't want stardust or formulae or ideology: she wants the plain old truth. Lou wants to work out *what on earth is going on*. Lou had her head in her hands and was leaning on the bonnet of her car. Her elbows were scrunched up underneath her, and she looked like she was trying to fold herself into one of those little triangles that people make out of crisp packets.

All the points of her jolted as a lady's voice said, 'Is your name Lou?' Lou looked up, her red cheeks had white stripes where her cold fingers had been pressing into her face. Her mouth hung open. Andrea was standing very close to her. She was dressed in a beige suit. Her face was open and intelligent. Her strong chin was noble. Her demeanour was friendly. Lou stared at her, registering the other woman's nice smell. Andrea hesitated politely, waiting for Lou to respond, and when she didn't, she continued, 'I understand that you can ... apparently you ... I mean ... you're Lou Arthur, right?' Andrea broke into a nervous smile, the words tripping out of her mouth, 'I mean, I already know who you are! The thing is, well...' For the first time in a long time, Lou Arthur felt the presence of joy. The two women maintained a level eye contact as Andrea finally got the words out: 'It's just that ... I hear it too.'

For a time it was as if the pair were the only two people in the universe. It was a blessed, passionate relief they found in finding each other. Andrea Barnfather had a slightly different story to Lou. She had managed to carry on functioning at work. Somehow her 'work mode' was strong enough to cleave her a path through the hum. But when she got home in the evening she would break down. She was enraged. Her husband left her, unable to take the endless investigations and the questioning. Andrea felt like he didn't believe her, although he said that he did. The truth was, she did not really mind that he left. She was already forgetting his face. Like Lou, Andrea had embarked on a furious search for the source of the hum; like Lou, she never located it. She found that it disappeared just before she went under the arches on Gloucester Road. It didn't dim, it just stopped. You could locate the boundary if you were careful. Although as soon as you were not hearing it you had an unnerving sense that you never did hear it in the first place. Not hearing it made you feel even more mad than hearing it did. *What have I been doing?* Sometimes the hummadruz didn't come *back* to Andrea until she was up the hill into Redland. She would be thinking *It's gone! It's gone!* But there it would be again.

Now they had each other Andrea and Lou both redoubled their efforts. Of course, the really clever move was to reach out to others. They pinned up a poster advertising a public meeting all around Westbury-on-Trym. It was this poster that eventually led them to the guru of the hum himself, Mr Stephen Pinkleton of Coombe Dingle.

✳ ✳ ✳

The public meeting initially seemed like a disaster. They had arranged thirty chairs in a circle in the hall but only six people turned up. I will describe them in the order they arrived. Firstly, there were two older ladies already waiting outside the door when Andrea and Lou arrived to set up. When asked if they heard the hum they replied enthusiastically 'Oh yes!' but neither of them could expand on the topic further. Arriving on the dot were two men in their twenties from the West Country UFO Research Association (WCUFORA). When asked if they could hear the hum, one of the men stayed silent and the other hesitated then said, 'Sometimes,' but at such a reduction of volume from his normal voice that no one felt they could acknowledge it. Lou became quickly enraged with the men's string of theories, which, among other things, related the hum to weaponry changes spearheaded by the Interplanetary Corporate Conglomerate; took it as proof of the Breakaway Civilisation thesis, possibly involving a meta-base below Filton Aerodrome; and understood it as the initial

stage of a Government Mind Control experiment targeting those most easy to manipulate. Lou asked them to leave,
which for some reason the men took as further proof of their
various hypotheses. They exited with some aplomb, tugging
at the lapels of their cheap suits as they did so. The penul-
timate arrival was more promising: a young woman with
matted blue hair who seemed to know all about the hum.
However, she resented Andrea and Lou's barrage of questions
and became first evasive and then rude. At a certain point
she stood up, kicked a chair across the room, and exited the
meeting with angry tears charging down her face.

Lou sighed. She and Andrea looked around the room. Lou's
look to Andrea said, '*Close the meeting, it's a wash-out.*' But just
then a man appeared at the door. He was portly and short. He
wore round glasses and a grey suit made from thick tweed.
He stuttered a little, but nevertheless spoke confidently. 'What
you're hearing: I can hear it. There are more of us. There is a
group. You should come. The noise, it's r-real. We call it the
hu-hu-hummadruz.'

Brin Caffery had a particular character. At first meeting
he seemed shy and nervously acquiescent, but to know him
was to know a deeply pernickety and pathologically officious
man. Mr Caffery was one of those people who, in order to
have any place in the world at all, required of himself that he
be forever bothered and bothersome. Should he not have had
the hummadruz to keep him busy he would have certainly
have found some other subject of vexation. The man would
have been writing angry letters on behalf of an association
of footpath users maybe, or perhaps, just for fun, hunting for
mistakes in someone's application for planning permission.
But Mr Caffery could hear the hummadruz and his mania
to find the source had taken a different form to both Lou's
and Andrea's. He had penned letters to various authorities, national and provincial, at a rate of about three a day

for a period of no less than two years. He had not achieved much but was content at least with the string of denials he had wrung out of everybody from the water company to the power board. He was especially feared in Bristol City Council, and he had some key figures in such a state of exasperation that they were even considering giving in 102 to some of his demands, just in the hope that his ceaseless badgering would then relent, or at least change its pitch.

It was only when Mr Caffery met Stephen Pinkleton that his campaign developed any kind of rational end game. Pinkleton was a born leader; he had vision. Mr Caffery had only blindly attacked, but Pinkleton recognised that: a) they would never actually stop the hummadruz without finding the source and eliminating it; b) they would never find the source without expert help, and c) they wouldn't get any of that while they were still considered crackpots. He and Caffery began to work together. They soon found others. The group managed to get the hum talked about, and even a few national papers reported on it. It was the Bristolian dialect itself, which has a particular sense of humour, that named the hum the hummadruz. Pinkleton and his friends accepted the name, in the hope that their city might accept them in return. They even took to referring to themselves as hummers. Pinkleton was very firm with the hummers. No one was to peddle theories about the hummadruz, at least not publicly. They were trying to get expert help, not enter into a series of credibility-destroying conversations with the people from the WCUFORA. Pinkleton's idea was to focus on the suffering of the hearers only, and to use this suffering to lobby government. Their goal was a public investigation, by professionals, that would prove the existence of the hummadruz and locate its source. The hummers wanted science on their side.

And so it was that Lou and Andrea were taken up to Pinkleton's place in Coombe Dingle. He had been a hummer for over a decade, and he suffered debilitating migraines. Mr Caffery whispered these things as he let them into the house with his key. They went into the living room. The curtains were drawn and the room was dark. Pinkleton was lying flat on the sofa, a damp flannel over his eyes. As they entered he very carefully folded it twice and placed it on the coffee table. He then took the earplugs out of his ears, packed them away into a small case, and placed this next to the flannel. He asked his guests to sit. He looked at Lou and Andrea and smiled. He spoke quietly but assuredly. His voice was kind. He told them his story and he told them the story of the hummadruz, such as he knew it. Here was a man acutely aware of the hum, and who was not ashamed or paranoid or irrational. Lou felt herself bubbling with emotion and relief. She looked over at Andrea, whose eyes were wet too. It became too much for Lou. She clutched her ears to give herself a moment's respite from the noise and allowed the tears to flow. Stephen stopped talking. He nodded slowly, like he had been waiting for her to cry. He looked at Lou with deep understanding and handed her a Kleenex from an unboxed pile in front of him.

When Lou had composed herself, he continued:

Never listen to they doctors. Don't tell 'n in the first place, and don't listen to what they has to say if oo already did. They want to lock it away in your head and make it all yours like. But taint: tiz real. They'll give a babber drugs to shut a babber up, but the hummadruz 's real. People don't want to know. Not yet. But ee's spreading. More hear it every time, see? It goes and it comes. It comes for a few month, then goes for a few more. Course, no one knows why. But this way we know it's real see, 'cos else why does me 'n Mr Caffery there hear it start up at the 'xact same time? Soon it will go, that's sure. But don't relax me babbers, because 'ee will be back. And when 'ee comes, then they'll be more hummers than ever. Mark my words: Coombe, Wesbree,

Enleaze, Clifton, Filton, Stoke Gifford… 'Ee's spreading. 'Ee'l spread as far as town next time praps. We hummers are only canaries in the mine, see. All peepaw'll hear it soon.

Pinkleton nodded gravely. 'That's why we've got to find the source, you see? It is the only way. Not jus fr'us, fr'everybody. For Brizzle.'

That morning in Coombe Dingle Lou and Andrea learned that the first recorded hearing was way back in the eighteenth century, when a naturalist (I fact-checked this and it is true – his name was Gilbert White) reported hearing a dull hum up on the Downs: 'Any person would suppose that a large swarm of bees was in motion and playing about his head,' wrote Gilbert in 1769. Pinkleton went on through history, giving mention to hummers notable and obscure, describing how each had done their bit to throw what light they could on the mystery of the hummadruz. In the nineteenth century the phenomenon even enjoyed a period of city-wide accept-ance, and was believed to be the sound of the world spinning.

∗ ∗ ∗

The hum left for some years, and then it returned. Just as Pinkleton had predicted, even more could hear it when it came back. In the early 1980s Bristol City Council, weighed down by the increasing number of complaints they were receiving about the hum (it remains unclear exactly what percentage Mr Caffery's correspondence accounted for), finally agreed to finance a public investigation.

Ashraf Bidawi and Phyllida Edgebaston were PhD students studying acoustics at Oxford University. Intrigued by the unusual request, they went down to Bristol with their equip-ment to run some experiments. Now, I should say that I do not understand the science of acoustics and I'm not going to research it *at all*. What I will do is tell you that after a fair bit of twiddling and fiddling with some chunky 1970s Dr Who-ish black boxes, Bidawi and Edgebaston found the hum. It was somewhere below 10hz, a hummer told me, along with some other technical information, from which all I took was the impression that the hummadruz is hard to find but out there, sort of, buzzing away to itself on some obscure bandwidth. Bidawi and Edgebaston were excited, for it should have been well below the range of human hearing and yet it did seem the hummers could hear it. But where was it coming from? Well, it was at the summit of this question that the investigation started to fall apart.

The scientists were set on an industrial explanation, and for various reasons this was deeply unpopular in certain quarters. You see, this was all taking place during our country's deeply traumatic period of deindustrialisation, when unemployment was skyrocketing and the council was fighting hard to maintain Bristol's proud tradition of industry. They didn't want the hummers' fanatical umbrage directed toward some workplace that hired over 1,000 skilled workers. To compound this, Pinkleton and many other hummers were skeptical about the explanation because they knew that the origin of the hummadruz *preceded* the country's deeply traumatic period of industrialisation. The effect of this was a war of words between the concerned parties and an eventual splitting of the hummer group that had formed around Pinkleton. Poor old Bidawi and Edgebaston must have wondered what they had got themselves into as they were cajoled and attacked in writing by Mr Caffery, and scuppered and thwarted at many turns by Bristol City Council. But the real tragedy of the situation was that the faultline passed right between Lou Arthur and Andrea Barnfather.

Andrea had taken a real liking to the scientists. Phyllida was younger than her, but capable and smart. She didn't let anything faze her. She was always climbing on rooftops, lugging equipment up hills and squinting into the rain. She was quiet, but when she spoke it was with a confident thoughtfulness. Andrea was inspired. So when Phyllida and Ashraf began to narrow the search down to industrial Avonmouth, Andrea was sold on the thesis. After all, this would perfectly explain why the hummadruz was only audible from the north and western parts of Bristol.

Lou, on the other hand, did not take to the scientists. She viewed the way that Andrea sided with the strangers from Oxford over Pinkleton, not to mention the amount of time she spent with them (she hadn't seen her properly in over a month), as nothing short of a betrayal. It was ridiculous to suggest that it was an industrial noise. That would mean it would be only audible in the daytime, or at least would be shut down occasionally. And why would it disappear sometimes for years at a time?

Phyllida, Andrea and Ashraf set out, the scientists laden with equipment of various kinds and wearing giant headphones, and Andrea looking sporty in a very fetching jogging suit. They approached the source in a straight line, looking more at the little winking monitor screens in front of them than what was under their feet as they scrambled through bushes, leapt over ditches, and scuttled across the giant lots of factories and processing plants. As they got closer and closer, they were surprised to find that the hummadruz got quieter and quieter, until, as they approached the source, it almost disappeared.

It turned out to be coming from a warehouse. It looked to be abandoned. Andrea and Ashraf kept watch as Phyllida kicked open a rusty side door to allow them in. Inside was dark. As their eyes adjusted to the light they saw, to their surprise, that it was completely empty. Andrea could hear nothing, but somehow she felt the hum's presence. A great sense of peace filled her. She had found the source. She felt safe, like she had evaded the hummadruz's teeth by climbing upon its back.

The three walked around and around the place, and Andrea listened with admiration to Phyllida and Ashraf unfolding their thesis. On the side of the factory next to the warehouse was a giant fan. They were told by the foreman that it was never shut off. Andrea excitedly confirmed that the noise it made did have something of the hummadruz to it. Of course, the fan was much louder and more distinct, but the sounds were the same pitch, even if the hummadruz itself was many octaves lower. It was Phyllida who surmised it first: the noise from the fan was bleeding into the empty warehouse (the windows were all broken), reverberating the entire structure, and then booming out across the land. The warehouse was acting like a giant speaker, bathing the people of Avon, North Somerset and South Gloucester in a low humming noise.

The hummers were split. Among those who supported the scientists' finding, there was a radical splinter cell who claimed that anyone who *doubted* the Avonmouth Thesis was being bribed or blackmailed by Bristol City Council. They claimed that the factory belonged to that venerable old secret society and locus of many a conspiracy theory, the Society of Merchant Venturers, and that this group was calling on contacts, pulling strings, intimidating people, and generally endeavoring to stop the truth from coming out. And it is certainly true that the council vociferously refused to accept the findings. And, of course, the council's refusal to do anything about the factory exaggerated the chagrin of the hummers. Andrea and Lou had a tearful argument up at Goram's Chair. Lou had got a dog, Hercules, and Andrea was accompanying the two on a walk. They stopped to look at the view. They could feel the tension between them about to snap. Lou was crying before it was even mentioned. The clouds above were heavy with rain. Andrea couldn't see why Lou wouldn't see sense. They had searched for so long, and now they had finally found the source. They were so close: they could stop the hummadruz! Lou could only hear the hummadruz and her own sobs. She and Hercules went home alone.

A few nights later, the Avonmouth fire service were called to extinguish a fire in an industrial district on the south end of town. As the sirens were sweeping toward the plume of black smoke rising above the town, a few figures, clad in black jumpsuits, could be seen disappearing into the scrub.

The next morning Andrea woke up with an incredible lightness in her heart. Last night seemed like a blur. She had slept on the sofa so as not to wake Phyllida, who was in her room. She knew she would be waking soon, and Andrea got up to make some coffee. As she hopped up off the sofa she looked out the window, and it was then that she noticed it. She rubbed her eyes. Her hands were still dirty. She opened the window and put her head out just to check. Her jaw fell open. Hot tears filled her eyes. She felt like screaming. Only when Phyllida appeared behind her did she realise that she *was* screaming. She fell into the scientist's arms. She could still hear the hum. The hummadruz was still there.

* * *

Fictional stories generally conform to a few established structures, and nearly all of them rely on the building of tension to some kind of climax – someone gets rich, or someone gets happy, or someone gets their comeuppance; a bomb is defused or a bomb goes off; someone dies to save someone else or someone ends up in someone's arms. Real life, however, doesn't always fit into such prescribed patterns. More's

HE DREADED HUMMADRUZ

107

the pity for this book, for I'm afraid to say that a clear resolution regarding the fate of these wretched hummers is going to continue to evade us. Even today, many simply refuse to believe that the hum exists outside of the hummers' heads. However, this is not to say that the centuries' old hummer battle against denial and ignorance has not had its victories. As more and more hummers have come out of the woodwork the sound has become harder to ignore. Hummers have embraced new technology. There's an app that can locate the hum and show people a visual representation of it. Social media has been a great conduit to bring hummers together:

> 'NO you are not mental. NO you are not going bonkers. If the noise bothers you, record it, screen shot it, fill in your forms and present the evidence to your local authority. Keep at it, even if you are the only one in your family who can hear it.'

> 'Make up a form on your computer with enough spaces to show time, date, Hz and dB readings and a comments column. You can write things in like *CAN'T SLEEP driving me crazy* or *steady dull drone which fills my head* or *two-tone noise which destroys sleep* etc., etc.'

Sufferers find each other quickly online, and once they are together they can organise. In 2003 the Department for Environment, Food and Rural Affairs (DEFRA) confirmed the existence of 'Low Frequency Noise', although they failed to allocate any funding to investigate where the disturbance may be coming from. Luckily, various scientists and pseudo-scientists have filled the gap, and over the years since Lou Arthur first began her search for the source, theories and explanations have proliferated. A scientific theory, however technical, is essentially a piece of storytelling, and a synopsis of some of the most entertaining will serve as a close to our tale.

Those investigations with a bent toward conspiracy theory often trace the sound to Filton Aerodrome. However, neither British Aerospace nor Airbus have ever let anyone investigate the site and so the thesis has been impossible to confirm or deny. This, of course, makes it all the more alluring.

Windy New Age types commonly ascribe the hummadruz to ley energy, pointing out that to the north-west of Bristol lies a point of convergence of two great ley lines: the Malvern Ley running south from Worcestershire meets the 'Perpetual Choirs' line, which, of course, runs south-east to north-west, starting at Stonehenge, passing through the Lansdown camp in Charlcombe, and presumably moving on to somewhere pretty mystical in Wales.

Other theories place the source of the hummadruz far, far away from Bristol, and then posit that the sound reaches us by reflecting off the ionosphere in a process of 'refraction'. The hummadruz in these cases is usually held to be a kind of weapon: a destabilising beam of sound directed at the city of Bristol by her enemies.

A slightly wackier theory, favoured by most of the scientific establishment, is that the hummadruz is the cumulative sound of thousands upon thousands of mating calls. The male Midshipman fish lets out a low drone when searching for a mate. The fish are incredibly adaptable but are particularly fond of underground caverns and caves. Their courtship call is famously loud, and the sounds that both sexes emit during intercourse are louder still. What is more, the fish mate pretty much continuously during their mating season, which comprises around nine-tenths of the year.

The most recent theory, and I have to say my personal favourite, is authored by two scientists from Bordeaux. Karel de Parfait and Fabien Fabien, senior scientists at the Centre National de la Recherche Scientifique, heard about the hummadruz after clicking on an alluring sidebar story on a popular acoustics news site. They were intrigued and flew to Bristol to investigate. The theory they cooked up relates to high-pressure waves continually beating at the floor of the Severn estuary. This in itself is not an uncommon oceano-graphic phenomenon, but because of various geographical peculiarities that run along the Avon, these high-pressure waves turn into *seismic* waves that travel through the land itself. As these waves reach Bristol, they meet a city that is pretty much hollow underneath, due to the incredible volume of underground tunnels, caverns and caves that exist beneath our feet. The seismic waves then reverberate in these underground spaces, vibrating the city above.

Now, I'm aware some of you are not that fond of the tune, but you have to admit that the theory in itself is pretty cool: that Bristol – the actual town, all the buildings and everything they are built on – is one massive speaker with the bass turned up too loud.

THE BAMBOO CLUB

DON'T HAVE SPACE to cover all of Bristol's pubs, clubs, cafés, night haunts and so on, so I'm going to pick one and stick with it. Naturally I am more than a little sorry not to be talking about Dutty Ken, owner of the Star & Garter, sacking his long-suffering employee Mark Dub eighteen times – or, for that matter, the time the punters crowdfunded his VAT bill. Of course, it's a shame not to talk about the night Ki Longfellow and Vivian Stanshall rocked up at the mud docks on *The Old Profanity Showboat*, which later became the *Thekla*. Also – keep your hair on – I am aware that every one of your local boozers has accrued legends like a ship collects barnacles, or else developed them like an old man does hairy warts and liver spots. However, cry as you might, I've made my choice: I'm going to talk about what is surely Bristol's most legendary venue, indeed one of the most legendary venues in the world: the Bamboo Club of St Paul's. If you've heard two things about the old place, they are probably that Bob Marley played there twice. It is a venue that died young, burning to the ground in 1977, having only been open a decade or so. As sad as this is (and indeed a whole community depended on the Bamboo Club for more than just good times) the place's brevity is somehow part of its immortality. It's something like those stars who die aged 27 (Joplin, Hendrix, Cobain, Winehouse – the list goes on): had they lived their stories would have been muddied and compromised, just like mine and yours. But leaving this world early, in flames no less, means that the Bamboo Club has been preserved perfectly in legend, with every bottle just where it was, and Desmond Dekker's arresting voice still hanging sweetly in the air.

The place was opened and run by Tony and Lalel Bullimore, and a nicer pair of people you couldn't hope to meet. They'll tell you themselves that the Bamboo was dreamed up in the blusies of St Paul's. Their friends pressed the mixed-race couple to open a venue where all people would be welcome, for this was a time where West Indians were barred from many establishments. It was a top idea, and the couple will go down in history as running one of the finest little venues in the world. They put on all sorts, but specialised in bringing over artists from Jamaica, playing bluebeat, rocksteady, ska and reggae. The list of stars that stood on the stage there is too immense for me to do justice to here, but includes Desmond Dekker, Laurel Aitken, John Holt, Derrick Morgan, The Skatalites, Jimmy Cliff, The Mighty Diamonds, Joe Tex, Lee Dorsey, Ben E. King and Percy Sledge. But it wasn't only about the music: the Bamboo served delicious food; they had a cricket team, a darts team, a football team and a dominoes team, all of them formidable. The Bullimores and others at the Bamboo helped many, many people, particularly West Indians, in a decade that was exceptionally hard on that community. It was a centre of mutual aid, a place where the good times just kept on coming, and one of the only mixed venues in a divided city.

I'll tell you how the place was eventually destroyed, but first let's hear about the time it survived destruction. The second occasion that Bob Marley played the venue – with the Wailers this time – there was a bomb scare. The police came and told Tony and Lalel that the club would have to be evacuated. The thing is, the crowd was already baying for Bob and the band. The show was running late because the band's gear had been caught in heavy snowfall on its way from London. Unfortunately, Bob's fame had already reached the point where it had started to bring out alarming psychotic behaviour in the fans. It wasn't just the usual crowd: people had been queuing round the block. Now they were demanding their money back. When poor old Tony went out to placate them he got a barrage of abuse. 'The bomb scare is probably connected to this lot,' thought poor Tony. He pictured himself being garrotted by an enraged Bob Marley fan. Tony tried to talk to the crowd, but they wouldn't listen to a word he said.

The worst thing was that the gear had arrived just before the police, and the band was ready to play; but Tony was going to have to tell the crowd that they had to evacuate. It makes you glad not to have fans, this kind of thing. Enthusiasm can be very scary in the wrong doses. Then Lalel had an idea. Bob should go and break the news! Bob, an absolute legend, said he was up for giving it a shot. Of course, the crowd went wild when he got on stage, but they obediently followed him out-side when he asked them to, coming up the stairs behind him like a wave of puppy dogs. The bomb disposal team rushed in as poor Bob was swamped. The man signed autograph after autograph while the police completed their search. Eventually they informed Tony and Lalel that their establish-ment had the all-clear. Bob and the Wailers returned back inside, followed by a distinctly larger crowd than had been there previously. Tony and Lalel wondered what they should do. There were over 200 people in a small venue, pushing it way over capacity. The couple looked at the faces of the crowd, all so happy to be rammed in there, close enough to Bob to touch him. They decided, wisely I believe, to let it rest and enjoy the music along with everyone else.

* * *

There is another good story concerning that very same show. Some of you won't remember the time when there was only vinyl and tapes. Back then certain recordings could be very rare indeed. There were fabled recordings that people had only ever heard tell of, or even some that not everyone believed in. The *Bob Marley and the Wailers at the Bamboo Club Live* tape was such a recording.

It did actually exist, in a manner of speaking anyway, and people paid good money to get a hold of it. By the time people were hearing the recording, the Bamboo Club itself had burnt down, and so to listen to it was to really hear a slice of Bristol history. Years went by and eventually anybody who was anybody had procured a copy. But then one day a young DJ called Jada Bouresh got hold of the famous tape and, upon listening to it, was struck by something. Jada was something of an aficionado, and she knew Marley's back catalogue well. The tape reminded her of something. She leafed through her record collection. Sure enough, it turned out to be Bob Marley live at the Rainbow Theatre in London, just played at a slightly slower speed. The people of Bristol had been duped, clamouring for a bootleg that was freely available at any record store. Jada leaned back onto her beanbag and smiled. It did sound nice on the tape, that was for sure. But then, a bit of Bob always sounds nice.

✳ ✳ ✳

There are conflicting reports as to why the Bamboo burned down. As usual the most sensational is also the most believable and relates to the concert that was scheduled for just a few days after the place was destroyed: The Sex Pistols. The legend goes that a neo-Nazi group were so outraged that 'white' music should be played in a 'black' club that they torched the place.

Should these idiots have been at the original punk venue, London's Roxy, they would have known that the only music the DJs would play between acts, and any self-respecting punk would countenance listening to, was Jamaican bluebeat, rocksteady, ska and reggae.

11
GHOSTS

WHY ARE THERE ghosts? It sometimes happens that a certain tale cannot quite become unattached from where it took place; a building may hold onto the story or the story onto the building. In some cases, you'll find that a ghost is a tale so large and misshapen that it cannot be contained solely in the world of story, and part of it pokes awkwardly out into the world of matter. In others it's the case that all concerned can see that someone's story has not ended with death, and that their spirit must continue to play a role though their body has returned to dust. Have a read of these spooky Bristol ghost stories and I hope you'll see what I mean.

The Odeon Cinema

In the film of Rudyard Kipling's novel *The Light that Failed*, there is a scene in which five shots are fired. At the premier screening of the film at Bristol's Odeon Cinema in 1946, a sixth shot was heard. No one in the audience noticed the discrepancy, putting the slight mismatch between the visuals and the audio to poor editing. However, the next day the cinemagoers were shocked to read in the papers that they had been present at a murder. The cinema's manager, the dashing Robert Parrington Jackson, was found shot dead in the projection booth of screen 3. The police have never solved the case and the weapon used to dispatch the man was never found. Whoever it was must have known the film and timed their entry into the booth, and the firing of the deadly bullet, so that the murder was masked by the on-screen action.

It always makes me laugh when people say that stories are there to brighten up a dull life, for surely it is the exact opposite: a story's role is to soften and obscure the truly sinister tales that are unfolding around every corner and behind every door. Robert Jackson is perhaps a good example of this himself. His beautiful clothes, boot-polish hair and charming anecdotes of his time in Hollywood are rumoured by some to have masked an alarming penchant for sexual predation. If this is true, it seems likely that the murderer was an avenging recipient of Jackson's unwanted advances – or else his own long-suffering wife.

What is sure is that Jackson has haunted the cinema ever since he was gunned down. He has a habit of appearing to female employees when they happen to be alone, a habit that death has not made any less creepy. He also causes disturbances during films that he considers to be pretentious or boring: so, before you shout at the teenagers behind you, please have the decency to first check if it was Jackson who was throwing the popcorn about. The phantom's presence is always accompanied by a mysterious chill in the air, so take a scarf – particularly if the film you're going to watch is French.

Yes Ms M'Cready

Tony is a big man. He's very big and very strong. Tony is a very *corporeal* man. His shoulders are a mountain range, his torso looks like a giant's clenched fist, his hands look like huge, inflatable hands. Just a glimpse of Tony is quite enough to remind you that we are very much material girls living in a material world. And Tony is also corporeal in his beliefs. The man is very much wedded to the idea that 'this is all there is' and always subscribes to the most narrowly materialistic philosophies available. Dawkins and Hitchens make up his reading material, and fair play to the guy. Tony was, for many years, head of security at Bristol's Old Vic, and his scepticism was part and parcel of his no-nonsense approach to the job.

At the end of the day, when all the darling actors had gone off to get drunk at Renatos and the box office folk had gone home, it was Tony's job to lock up. He always used to do this in the company of his massive Alsatian dog, also called Tony. The Tonies would, both being very fastidious, do a round of the entire building, looking for anything out of place or untoward and locking all the doors. Now, one night they were downstairs, just about to finish the rounds, when they witnessed something that would rupture their entire worldview. You see, the last thing that needed to be done before leaving the building was to shut off all the power at the great bank of switches that resides in the corridor that goes around the side of the stalls. Tony would always have a torch with him so that after turning out the lights he and Tony could make their way safely back into the foyer and out.

So this one night they were on this final leg of the routine, just about to go back upstairs, when Tony felt a breeze. Assuming that this must mean that he had left one of the doors into the theatre open (which was very unlike him) he turned back to correct his mistake. But as he tried to move back down the corridor Tony started pulling on his leash in the direction of the exit. Tony, surprised by the uncharacteristic disobedience, tried to pull his colleague toward the stalls. Reluctantly, the dog gave up the tug of war and started up a low growl instead. The pair had only taken a few steps when they heard a voice say 'Get out!' It wasn't loud and sounded like it was being played at one remove, like it was on a recording perhaps. For a brief second Tony was frightened. He steeled himself – this was no time for the heebie-jeebies; some kids were obviously playing a prank. It was close to Halloween, after all. Tony started marching down the corridor and was just going to bark something threatening when suddenly he met with the overpowering scent of lavender. This was especially surprising for Tony the dog, who knew that if there had been a smell so sweet and potent in the building it should have registered from upstairs. The lavender had appeared out of nowhere and was unmistakable. The Tonies slowed. The voice spoke again. This time it was louder and clearer. Tony had the feeling like there was someone standing right in front of him. He could feel their breath on his face. He could hear the lips and the teeth at work. The words were very clearly articulated; the projection was strong – albeit not needed in a small corridor – the elocution excellent. This disembodied voice knew how to speak. 'GET OUT!' it repeated. It said it like it really, really meant it.

Those of you familiar with Bristol's ghosties will know that Tony had encountered the spirit of Ms M'Cready; the nineteenth-century actor, stage manager, security guard, manageress and single-handed saviour of the Old Vic. She can be recognised, in death as in life, by a potent smell of lavender. It precedes and outlasts every sighting of her. The Ms M'Cready tale is still told with much relish, and her ghost is sighted regularly. There are slightly trashy stories about her having a fistfight with Jane Austen, but my favourites concern her tenacious ability to keep the show going, even when it means running out and pressganging performers from among the patronage of The Old Duke. M'Cready couldn't let the venue go like she did life, and she still takes a keen interest in things today. For instance, it is said that she worked closely with the architect on a recent refurbishment programme. He has assured the current management that the old boss approves of the new look.

Familiar to the spirit, renowned raconteur and theatre employee Andrew Stocker's assessment of the Tonies' encounter was that old Ms M'Cready believed them to be patrons. You see, she used to do the security job herself back in her day, and she frequently had to turf ruffians and drunkards out of the theatre after a performance. Just like Tony, her last job of the night was going down the corridor, locking all the doors, and making sure she was the only soul left in the venerable Old Vic.

Room 160

In the eighteenth century, what is now the Arnos Vale Hotel used to be a famously strict school for girls run by famously strict nuns. These nuns were really strict, I can't emphasise that enough. Rumour has it that one of these strict nuns fell pregnant, due to an incident involving one of the students' fathers and a regrettable lapse of strictness. Upon finding out that she was pregnant, the rest of the Order settled on a rather extreme solution. They quarantined the sister by bricking her up inside a windowless, door-less cell. The solution was permanent, and both problems died in that little prison. For days the poor woman bloodied her fists pounding at the walls. She lost her voice from screaming. Who can say how long it took for her to die? All we know is that for over 100 years her body was encased in this secret chamber.

After the building was turned into a hotel, management began to log complaints from guests complaining of a muffled knocking noise that went on long into the night. Occasionally someone would come down to reception and insist that a woman in the next room was being attacked. Every time the employee on the nightshift would go up to check, they would find the occupants of Room 160 sound asleep. Apart from these anomalies being recorded in the hotel's handover notebook, the story of the trapped nun had become completely submerged in Bristol history and no one remembered anything about it.

Things were to change during the Second World War, when the Luftwaffe targeted St Philip's Marsh and dropped a few bombs up toward Brislington for good measure. One hit the hotel and the sister's hoary cell was blown open. Of course, the story was out then, and all of west Brislington was prattling about the skeleton found in the Arnos Vale Hotel. The chatter died down after a while, as it does, but the spooky activity did not. Ever since the hidden room was blasted open, guests have reported hearing a muttering voice, footsteps running down the corridor, moaning, wailing and crying. Occupants of Room 160 frequently report poltergeist activity: with baths being run and toiletries being flung across the room. Most terrifying of all, there have been several instances of attacks on sleeping people. Interestingly, all of the victims in these cases are women. They are pinned down by what feels like an immense pressure applied to their chest. Sometimes they also feel cold, wet hands enclosing their wrists or covering their mouths. As far as I am aware the victims of these horrid attacks never report seeing anything. However, there have been sightings in the room, too. The ghost is seen in a corner by the bathroom, naked and pacing round in pathetic little circles, tracing the outline of her old cell. Her head will hang morosely between her shoulders and blood will drip from where her fingernails once were.

Of course, the hotel has lost a lot of custom because of the ire of this afflicted spirit, although potential negative economic impact is counteracted by the burgeoning demand for 'paranormal tourism'. Much to management's delight, a steady stream of ghost-hunters and thrill-seekers have ensured that the permanent occupant of Room 160 is never alone for long.

The Hatchet Public House

Back in the 1970s the aptly named Hatchet pub in Frogmore Street was always full of bikers (or greasers as they were known then). It was before my time, of course, but I am told the pub was a real 'no go' area. There were punch-ups galore, and frequently improvised weapons would be brought into the fray. You see, the greasers considered using carried weapons to be somewhat uncouth, and anyone with decorum would simply grab what instruments were to hand when it came to fight time. Thus you hear stories of chair legs and motorcycle chains being utilised to terrific effect in the establishment's rollicking bar room brawls.

In previous centuries the Hatchet was frequented by the gnarliest pirates in all of Bristol, which, of course, means the gnarliest pirates in the entire world. The persistent rumour is that the door of the Hatchet is covered in human skin. The skin is meant to have been flayed off pirates by some other pirates (presumably as punishment for infractions against some piratical code) and then used to upholster the door. Whether this was as a warning or simply for convenience is not recorded. To be honest, I wouldn't be surprised if it is true. I did, of course, inspect the door, but one encounters only thick black exterior paint. One of the wizened old regulars, a chap called Dewayne Knoggin, explained to me the reason why no one has chipped away at the paint to look if there is indeed a layer or two of leathery old story under there: 'On the way in they needs a drink and on the way out they's too pissed!'

Another thing that the searcher out of curios may want to do is to look at the attic room, the one with the little window up in the roof. Tell me if you find out how to get there though, because even though the room is clearly visible from the outside I was unable to find it on the inside. They say that it has been bricked-up and then obscured by a new plaster job. I'm afraid the most likely explanation is tragic. A prostitute was said to have hung herself from the roof beams. For some reason no one wanted to deal with the poor woman's corpse, and the decision was made to brick up the little room from which she worked. The job was hastily done and the spirit has been trapped inside ever since. Unlike most coffins, however, this one has a window. Sightings of a figure at the little window are common. Someone who used to work in the Hatchet told me that she would occasionally see someone sitting by the window and looking out. Presumably the management of the Hatchet know where the little room is but are reluctant to see the spirit released and thus open themselves up to the same sort of paranormal activity suffered by the Arnos Vale Hotel.

Sally on the Barn

Now I've heard a lot of confused stories about this Sally. What's agreed is that she's a statue that stands atop an ancient barn near the river on Court Farm Road. From there on, accounts differ wildly. There are tales of her cavorting with Roman soldiers for instance, which are little more than salacious gossip if you ask me – and would mean that some Roman-era sculptor possessed a strange aptitude for early modern styles. Luckily for me I don't need to sort out the mess that Bristol has got this narrative in. If anything, my job is to confuse things even further.

First off, the teenagers of Longwell Green swear that Sally comes alive at night and drowns people in the nearby river by clutching onto them and plunging in. Sally is a large statue and you wouldn't have a hope in hell of staying afloat with her on your back. You would certainly die screaming in the freezing water, and the coroner would puzzle over the bruises when you washed up in Hotwells or St Philip's.

There are various origin stories for Sally. In one she was once a living woman in possession of a breathtaking voice. When the moon was full Sally liked to stand atop the old barn, look out over the Avon towards Keynsham, and belt out all manner of songs. There is something holy about someone who does not try to turn their gift into money or even social kudos, but instead gives it back in paeans to the bowing reeds and the milky stars above. Upon the wild troubadour's death, Longwell Green decided to commemorate her with a figure that they placed where she had so often stood and sung. Perhaps it is her free spirit that is still heard on moonlit nights, still serenading the grassy banks of the old river as it trundles through the darkness.

In another version, Sally was a girl who died protecting some hiding Cavalier soldiers from the Roundheads during the Civil War. They were all set on torturing the information out of her when she escaped their clutches and ran into the barn. They were hot on her tail as she went up into the top room and then through a trapdoor and onto the roof. Perhaps in a film she would have made the jump and landed in a convenient hay bale, but in reality she was shot down as she ran along the roof beam. Later, after the restoration of the monarchy, some grateful cavalier soldiers commissioned a statue to commemorate the young girl who had saved their lives during the war.

Another version of the tale is considerably darker. In this one the statue is moved or stolen from a church in Keynsham. The way I like to tell it, the statue had fallen in love with her sculptor, a passionate craftswoman of the early modern period whose name was never recorded. You'll see yourself that the look on Sally's face is one of intense possessiveness and longing. I found that if I stood where her gaze was directed I could not hold it and was forced to look away. The angel was originally placed on the church, as per the contract, and lived for Sundays when her beloved would pass below her into the sanctuary to worship, and then disappear off up the path back toward her workshop following the end of the service. When the sculptress died a tear appeared in the corner of the statue's left eye, and thanks to the perceptiveness of the Bristolian imagination, her creator was buried directly where the angel was eternally fixated.

There is only one word to describe Sally's reaction to being moved to a barn on the banks of the River Avon in Longwell Green: *rage*. She hates Longwell Green. Her only nourishment – locking her gaze upon the final resting place of the beautiful individual whom she loved – has been taken away. Now she watches the greasy Avon sliding by on its way to meet the dirty Severn and broods on all she has lost.

Who knows what the quality of Sally's character is really like? Bristol has not resolved the various legends to a single backstory. I tried to divine something myself, but Sally kept her stony thoughts to her stony self. Perhaps she sings to the moon *and* murders people walking home along the river at night. It is true that there are more drownings along that stretch than almost anywhere else. But then perhaps people in Longwell Green are just weak swimmers. Speaking personally, while I understand that Sally's singing could be worth the risk, I really don't want the last moment of my life to be spent trying to prise some stone arms from around my neck. For this reason I have no intention of walking down Court Farm Road at night any time soon.

12

A BOOK BOUND IN HUMAN SKIN

NOW OF COURSE, reader, you do understand that what I am writing here is a strange amalgamation. I was told by many about the infamous 'Book Bound in Human Skin', which is variously said to reside at Bristol Record Office, the Bristol Royal Infirmary, Bristol Museum and Bristol University – but which I eventually saw for myself at the wonderful M Shed. The stories about how this ghastly item came into being were even more diverse than the suggestions of its current residence. What I have done here is to unscrupulously brew a selection of what I gathered from people, plaques, books, blogs, vlogs, docs, pamphlets and such into a concoction that suits my own taste. I'm not alone in this, for turning history into story always involves conjecture and guesswork, and as such leaves ample room for bias. I suppose I could just dispassionately list the established facts of the case, the bones of the story if you will; but that would be boring, and I was specifically asked by the good people at The History Press to not write a boring book. No, it's far better that we dive into the murky depth of the story, which, after all, is where we will encounter the characters. For people do not live in facts, they live in stories – and more's the pity for them when it is a story such as this. Ladies and gentlemen, read on if you dare: this is the macabre tale of Bristol's *Doctor Death*.

* * *

There once was a boy called John Horwood. John lived in Jefferies Hill, Hanham, and liked nothing better than to sit on the thickly wooded banks of the Avon and dangle his fishing rod into the murky water. One spring Sunday in 1820, as John was headed down from the little cottage where he lived with his parents, he met a bonny young lass walking up the path toward him. Well, cupid must have launched one of his arrows, for John's knees quivered and his jaw slackened as he fell immediately in love with her.

John asked her a dozen questions in quick succession. She politely answered him as best she could, revealing that her name was Eliza Balsum and that she lived alone with her widowed mother in Hanham. Well, John didn't push a worm onto his hook that day but paced up and down the bank of the river unable to focus on anything but his thoughts of Eliza.

Now, there is disagreement about what happened over the next few weeks or so, but it does seem that Eliza and John did at least become friends – and it is clear that John always wanted more. Whether or not they kissed in the oak tree bed, or spent a night cuddled by the fire at old Miss Western's, was all hotly debated at the time, first in the way of gossip and then later in a court of law. These questions are still contested today, as our narrative will soon show, but to me it doesn't particularly matter. Smooch or no smooch, someone's getting made into a skin book at the end of this story. I'll leave the smooch up to you, dear reader: if you feel they smooched then by all means let them smooch.

The important thing is that Eliza began feeling a little uncomfortable. She was aware that John liked her in a way that she did not return, and such a situation is hardly dignified for either party. She repeatedly told him that she did not love him but considered him a friend, but John continued to bother her. Eliza's mother told her that she simply had to ignore the boy and his interest would soon wear off.

But it didn't. One day John asked Eliza that question commonly known as *The Question*, which is by far the scariest question anyone ever did ask: 'Will you marry me?' She declined the offer, but John was not going to give up so easily, and kept asking. At long last Eliza ran out of demureness and told John in no uncertain terms to leave her alone. This seemed to hit home, and John looked truly injured and bereaved. But though she pitied him, Eliza stayed firm. Over the next few weeks life went back to normal. But then one dull afternoon John happened to see Eliza in Hanham walking and talking with another boy. Again there was (and still is) speculation about the particulars of Eliza's relations with this young man – but again they do not matter; the key thing is that this was the moment that John's treasured illusions about Eliza's possible affections for him were shattered once and for all.

Unfortunately, this illusion was the only thing keeping Eliza safe, and from that day on John started to attack her. It's funny that our language has no male equivalent for the popular phrase *Hell hath no fury like a woman scorned*, because scorned men kill two women a week in our country. John became obsessed with hurting Eliza. He would throw stones at her whenever she came to Hanham. He would chase her through the street. When Eliza wasn't around he would harass her mother, promising to one day kill her daughter. Worse still, John had started hanging out with a bad crowd, Hanham's infamous Cockroad Gang, and they were only too happy to assist him with his persecutions.

This went on for a week or so, with Eliza trying her best to avoid John and the Cockroad boys. One day she had gone with a friend down to the brook to fetch a few pails of water. Avoiding the well that everyone else used, they decided it would be safer to go to the brook that runs down Conham Hill. They went along as inconspicuously as anyone could and quickly arrived at their destination. But somehow John Horwood was there waiting for them. He was clasping a rock in his fist. He stared at Eliza with confused hatred in his eyes. He believed her to be like a demon who had spent all eternity plotting to take away everything that was rightfully his. Eliza blinked. She wondered what she had ever done to make John so angry and how she could make amends. She trembled, on the verge of reaching out to him. The pail of water rattled and sloshed in her hand. The scene was played out in slow motion. Seeing her distress John deflated slightly, and for a moment it looked as if he was going to turn and leave. But then in a flash he had thrown the rock at her. It seemed barely to have left his fist when it slammed into her head, glancing up from her crown. She cried out and fell down into the brook.

Her friend managed to get her home, and then to the infirmary as quickly as she could. Eliza was admitted and taken to a surgeon of some renown, Dr Richard Smith. Initially it did not seem to the medical professionals that the injury would be too serious, but Dr Smith decided to have her stay for a few days in order to keep an eye on her. Upon hearing about the dastardly manner in which she had earned her injury, Dr Smith did something highly uncommon (although to be fair he was generally recognised as something of an eccentric genius): he decided to personally ensure that John was arrested.

On 26 January 1821, two officers were sent to the Horwood's house in Hanham. John's sister insisted on seeing their warrant, which they had not procured. They paid no mind and pushed past her, going upstairs. The first room they came to contained John's bedridden mother, who peeked over the covers at them with bloodshot eyes. The gentlemen turned back around just in time to see John coming at them with a hammer. He launched blow after blow upon them, cursing at them in the secret Kingswood tongue all the while. The two officers fought back with their truncheons and after a bloody tussle they finally overpowered John and bundled him into Dr Smith's private carriage. They clattered off toward Bristol, with John's mother and sister standing weeping in the doorway.

John was taken to the infirmary, where he met with the eminent doctor himself. Before I relate the details of this meeting, I must first introduce an important character into the story. She hails not from the early nineteenth century, but from our own times. Her name is Mary Halliwell and she is a descendent of the Horwoods. She unearthed John's story when researching her family tree. Intrigued, she and her husband Dave did some research into the case that they later published as a quite astonishing book. This book uncovers a great deal of evidence pertinent to John's case and ends up casting the murderer in a more sympathetic light than anyone else in the whole of Bristol has ever dared. Now, I can hear you already baulking at the thought that John should be let off the hook for his vicious assaults on poor Eliza. I too, at first, dismissed the Halliwells as a pair of amateurs trying to clear an ancestor's name for reasons of mere tribalism. But I beg you to hear them out. They do not deny that John did something horrible to Eliza, but they reveal that he was not the only one who deserves our disgust and judgement. They also give a level of contextual detail that I dare not match for fear you start thinking you're reading a history book.

The first thing that the Halliwells bring to our little account here is a proper description of the life up in Hanham and Kingswood during the early nineteenth century. The folk there were a fiercely independent lot, and almost exclusively worked in the mines that they dug and managed themselves. They spoke in their own dialect, ran their own worship, and educated their own children. It was no picturesque fairy tale up there, mind. The mining was incredibly dangerous. John's uncle had been killed, as had Eliza's father, and many others on an almost daily basis. Children were often taken to work at a young age, carried down to the pit on their father's backs. John's mother and father were good people, respected by others in the community, but John was a sensitive child and he had always hated being fed down the narrow shafts of the mines. When he was a young man he witnessed a tragic accident and was too traumatised to go back. His trauma destroyed his confidence. All the respected men in his community worked in the mines. He was probably deeply ashamed and felt himself an outcast. After dropping out he started misbehaving. This is when he started mixing with the Cockroad Gang, who made their money robbing folk on the road to Bristol. He would hang out with the boys at the Blue Bowl Inn, which still serves a decent pint of ale today, just as it did back when the Romans were ruling the roost in Bristol town. The awe-inspiring longevity and stability of an ancient establishment like that is a comfort to me, so Lord knows what it meant to the impoverished, option-starved young John Horwood. Back at home, John's mother was dying. He could not face reality, for reality was too painful. But the odd pint of ale at the Blue Bowl is not enough living for a young man. So once it came, his love for Eliza was the one thing that made sense to him in the whole world. This does not excuse what he did, but it does help explain it.

* * *

The details of the meeting between Dr Richard Smith and the boy John Horwood I shall relate in a moment, but first I should explain a little more about the doctor. You will have already got a sense of his commitment to his work, but let's further admire the details of this learned man's passion for medicine and human anatomy. While we are at it, I'll endeavour to explain to you why I think Smith well deserves the title of Bristol's *Doctor Death*.

You see, the doctor was a performer of Public Anatomisations, which in those days presented a very popular evening out for well-to-do ladies and gentlemen, as well as teaching doctors and medical students a great deal about human anatomy. Because of the popularity of these Public Anatomisations, there was a premium on corpses at the time. A body in decent nick was worth around £6, which was a great deal of money in the early 1800s. Naturally, there were folk who would readily dig freshly buried bodies from the grave for such a reward. Those who did so were known as body snatchers or Resurrection Men. The doctors themselves were not shy of taking corpses themselves where they thought they could. In fact, the annals of Bristol record that some officers one night caught a group of doctors digging up a woman who had been buried earlier that day.

However, Dr Smith had an alternative method of getting hold of bodies. You see it was he who had the job of performing autopsies for the court in cases where cause of death needed to be established. In return for this service, the city authorities allowed the doctor to take the bodies of executed criminals and use them how he wished. Desiring the income and the medical experience that public anatomisations brought him, Dr Smith always took a keen interest in any case that may result in a hanging. The public's interest in criminology was as insatiable then as it is now, and the accepted view was that murderousness and violence resided somewhere in the body, and for this reason people paid good money to watch Dr Smith search for it with his scalpel and his hacksaw. Recognising the crowds' interests and appetites, Smith even took it upon himself to compose little poems about his co-stars' nefarious exploits. Over his career he composed hundreds of ditties that detailed the lives and misdeeds of the various criminals who had lain upon his table.

On top of this, the good doctor was also something of a collector. His house was chock-full with skulls, toes, pelvises, ribs, organs preserved in great jars of formaldehyde, elbows, knuckles, dried ears, kneecaps, teeth and so on. Smith liked to keep a memento from every one of the criminals he dissected. Should you have been invited to his house for dinner, he may well have taken the opportunity to let you hold a femur or a jawbone while he recited some poetry concerning its erstwhile owner. Rather than despising him for such practices, Bristol recognised Smith as a man of science, and indeed he held the venerable title of 'Master of the Royal Secret' in the Royal Sussex Lodge of the Freemasons.

* * *

It is my hope that you now have sufficient background to be let in on what occurred between John Horwood and Dr Richard Smith when the former was first arrested and dragged to the infirmary to meet with the latter. You see the boy was taken in, and, being a poor boy who never left Hanham, he was most disturbed to be trapped in the office of a distinguished Bristol luminary. It is perhaps understandable that he began to act up, replying to Dr Smith's questions in the most vulgar ways he could. For a while the doctor continued with his interrogations, but, making no progress, he tried a different tack. He began, to John's surprise, to recount the story of two notorious child killers who had been caught in their vile crimes and executed by the city. John, along with every other Bristolian, had of course heard of them, for the more horrible the news the better it spreads. John sat in confused silence as Dr Smith described in detail the two killers and their inexplicable acts. Looking into John's eyes all the while, the older man walked calmly over to a curtain rail and pulled it back. The moment he saw the two skeletons, John's stomach lurched and he tried to flee the room. One of the officers present pushed him firmly back into his seat.

Having quietened John in this ingenious manner, the doctor continued with his plan, taking the boy onto the ward to see Eliza. Now, this must have been terrifying for her, but Dr Smith assured her that she was safe and asked her to identify the man who had tried to kill her. She was brave enough to motion at John, although she wouldn't look at him. John stayed morose and quiet throughout this awkward little interview, although he did at one point deny that he had been trying to kill her.

Dr Richard Smith was now quite sure that John was the attacker, and the boy was thrown in Bridewell jail. Soon after, Eliza Balsum died due to complications after receiving surgery at the hands of Dr Smith. The latter stated (under oath in court no less) that she had developed an abscess on the outer table, and that by his estimation she needed trepanning. Trepanning is the most ancient of all the surgeries, going back 10,000 years or more, and is the practice of drilling of a hole in the skull to release pressure on the brain. Unfortunately, this time it did not work, and although she initially survived the procedure, Eliza died a few days later.

* * *

Let's return to Mary Halliwell's work. John's descendant dug up some illuminating new information regarding Eliza's death. You see, following the autopsy, Dr Smith had kept Eliza Balsum's head. He had no right to do this so far as I know, and whether he gave the family an explanation, or simply got the mortuary to cover the body so they would not notice, is unknown. However Smith procured it, Eliza's skull is to play a pivotal role in the Halliwells' thesis. Dr Smith had such a number of these gruesome keepsakes that he had them labelled. For this reason, many years after he was gone, it was possible to re-examine Eliza's injury. It was discovered that the cause of Eliza's death was not the original blow to the head, nor an 'abscess on the outer table' as Dr Smith claimed in court. Rather, what killed the girl was the operation he performed: one that does not even appear to have been necessary. Of course, this could all be but human error on the doctor's part. But the Halliwells' ask you to consider motivation: Smith knew that if Eliza died then John would be executed, and he would have the body of a murderer to publically dissect. He could continue the pioneering investigations into the 'criminally insane' that were the source of his celebrity. The Haliwells' insight has been to point out that in the sad case of John Horwell and Eliza Balsum, it was in the doctor's interest that Eliza should die, thus making John a murderer. This would ensure that he would be given the body first of Eliza, to ascertain cause of death, and then of John, when, as part of his sentence, his body was given up to Public Anatomisation. Dr Smith went down with a good name; against this official history, the Halliwells claim that he was a liar, a body snatcher, and a cold-blooded killer.

* * *

John Horwood was found guilty of murder at a trial that took place in a pub in Bedminster. The case of the defence was very weak indeed, and it soon collapsed. Eighteen-year-old John was sentenced to death by hanging.

John's mother was a Methodist, as were many others from Hanham and Kingswood, but he himself didn't know the first thing about religion. A minister came to him in his cell where he awaited his death and reminded him that in 24 hours he would be finding out whether there really is an afterlife. It was advisable, said the minister, to lay down now any burden that you did not want to take there, so as to be travelling light should your spirit find the hypothesis to be correct. John was feeling like he couldn't carry his burden for another 24 hours anyway, let alone for eternity, and so it was that he tearfully confessed his hideous crime, in which he had transmuted love to hatred, and persecuted then killed an innocent person.

After talking with the minister for a long time, John found that he had got religion. He begged the man to do what he could to improve conditions at Jefferies Hill – for even in just this little glimpse of Bristol, with its well-fed people in pretty clothes, revealed to him what a shameful mire of hunger and distress his people lived in.

John's mother was too sick to visit, but the rest of his family came. 'His countenance bespoke the anguish of his heart,' wrote the minister, who accompanied the family. He went on to relate how John's sister buried her face in his neck, weeping 'O my dear brother!' – and how John was too deeply affected to make a reply. His old, grey-haired father wept, 'What? To die tomorrow!' His brother dragged John down to his knees, so that they could pray together. John wept, 'Do you think He could save me?' and his brother replied, 'Yes, you are the very character... He died for the vilest of the vile. And God accepts of a broken heart.'

John spent a long time with the minister that night, and early in the morning he asked to be left alone to think.

* * *

Due to the promotional activities on the part of Dr Smith, a great number of well-to-do ladies and gentlemen had come to Bridewell with the hope of meeting the condemned before the execution, so as to get a look at him alive before they saw him on the slab later that evening. John was taken to meet them. I imagine they were in the prison governor's office. The gentlemen probably stood around the walls smoking while the ladies stood whispering and hushing each other in a great bunch in the middle. Being introduced to high society is (I imagine) nerve-wracking at the best of times, and for an uneducated gang member who is about to be executed it must have been terrifying. But by the sound of it John dealt with the situation admirably. Our account of this odd little meeting comes from none other than Dr Richard

Smith himself. He relates that, after standing awkwardly and absorbing the stares, John went around the room shaking everybody's hand in turn. Smith relates how he hid behind some other gentlemen in order that John would not see him. You see, Smith was there waiting to collect the body after the execution and was worried lest, 'my errand might flash across his mind.' Once John had introduced himself, he suggested to the room that they pray together. The gentlemen did little more than look sheepishly at the carpet, reluctant to take religious queues from a condemned pauper. Some of the women though, more sensible to the ironies of such spiritual haughtiness, were moved to kneel with the boy and pray.

Smith's reflection on this little scene, as recorded in his diary, was that one of the praying women probably had some experience in public speaking, based on her 'easy flow of words'. I have spent a long time wondering, from right back when I first saw the Skin Book in the M Shed, if Dr Smith was a psychopath. Reading his diary, I'm not so sure he was. I think a psychopath would have been curious to show himself to John at that moment, would take a measure of delight in the grotesqueness or the fear. I think the truth was that Smith wasn't even thinking about John that much. I think that he simply did not see what he was doing as that morally dodgy or unfair. I don't think him, or many others in his echelon of society, really cared at all about the lives of the people of Hanham and Kingswood. Whether they lived or died did not matter and, should there be half a reason for them to die, then they may as well die.

* * *

John stood on the gibbet before the large crowd who had assembled to watch his execution and told them that he was guilty. He had only meant to hurt Eliza with the stone but had threatened to murder her often enough. He had never been entitled to anything in his life, but he had somehow convinced himself he was entitled to the life of one of the fairest creatures upon the earth. He had lost himself in his frustration and hurt, and now a woman was dead. He also confessed to many robberies, including from his dear parents, who had always stayed honest even when they were half-starved. He told the crowd the bitter lesson that he had learned. It is one still worth heeding: 'If you do not break off your bad habits, the end will be bad.'

After his speech all the sheriffs and officers were weeping. Dr Smith had left the room and gone to loiter by the stairs, like a butcher's boy who turns away from the bungled slaughter of a calf. The hangman had disappeared too, no longer wanting to do his job and execute John Horwood. But the audience was waiting: they had bought their snacks and their sensationalist accounts of Horwood's crimes, and the law had to be fulfilled before their eyes. The authorities composed themselves and took their places around the gibbet. John closed his eyes in prayer for a moment, then dropped his handkerchief; this being the sign that he was ready. His sister cried out. His father made a broken noise. The body jolted as the rope snapped taught, then swung lifeless in the noose.

* * *

Through the Methodist churches and John's parents, the people of Hanham had got wind of the doctor's determination to cut John up and leave nothing for a funeral. John's parents had begged him to at least leave them something that could be interred at a proper Christian burial, but he had politely refused. It seemed a potent symbol of the way that those out at Hanham and Kingswood got treated by those from town, and so a large number of miners assembled outside Bridewell to try to rescue the body. They stood around the court and waited for it to be moved.

However, Smith had caught wind of this. He dressed John up in the clothes of a gentleman, put a top hat on him, wrapped him in a cloak, and put him in a regular cab with a lady either side of him. A few miners peered into the cab as it left the court but saw only a young gentleman asleep upon his mother's shoulder.

∗ ∗ ∗

Dr Smith anatomised the criminal in a lecture hall in the Bristol Royal Infirmary before a crowd of eighty gentlemen, gentlewomen and medical professionals. John was disembowelled, with each organ taken out one by one. The top of his skull was carefully sawn off, and his brain was removed. Before the body was carried away (so that the flesh could be boiled away to reveal the skeleton) Dr Smith removed as much of the skin as he could.

The skeleton was articulated and placed in Smith's office with the others. He showed the skull to a phrenologist friend of his, who apparently confirmed popular opinion: 'Oh brutal, brutal... It has all the animal propensities.' The doctor took the skin and carefully tanned it, using a solution of salt and bark and urine, over a period of six weeks. He did a remarkable job considering that no tanner could advise him on how best to preserve human skin. Once the process was complete, Smith sent the skin to a book binder, who was instructed to use it to bind a collection of papers relating to John's case – including, of course, Smith's own poem relating to the matter. The cover of the book was embossed with a skull and the words *Cutis Vera Johannis Horwood* (The Actual Skin of John Horwood) were there inscribed in letters of gold. The book was the crowning achievement in a career packed with macabre theatrics.

* * *

The minister who had met John in jail remembered his promise. Firstly, a memorial service was held on Jefferies Hill, which was where the faithful of Hanham gathered on a Sunday anyway, in the shade of the trees atop the hill. The minister organised a giant marquee along with tea and sandwiches. Around 2,300 people turned up, but somehow there was ample to go round, with enough crusts left over to keep the dogs happy. They held the service for John and Eliza both. Outside it hailed furiously, a million icy pellets flinging themselves onto the canvas above them. The proceedings were halted because nobody could hear. The congregation sat still and listened. It sounded like the sky was tearing.

Soon afterwards a church was built in that spot – Christchurch Jefferies Hill – which stands there to this day. And it is in this church that the story finds its end. You see, for years John's body had been left hanging in a cupboard under some stairs at the university. That is until Mary Halliwell, as his descendent, won the right to finally give her forebear a proper burial. The university reluctantly handed John's skeleton over to the Halliwells, who had arranged a hearse and a proper funeral procession, such as a poor boy from nineteenth-century Hanham could never have expected. John Horwood was interned next to his father on 13 April 2011, exactly 190 years, to the very hour, after he was hung. The rain poured down on the mourners, the journalists, and everyone else in Hanham and Kingswood.

When Dr Smith died in 1843 at the age of 71, a respected Bristol paper wrote: 'Bristol has lost one of her most devoted sons, and best and brightest ornaments.'

13 CRIME

John Cabot and the Great Deception

Poor old John Cabot. He came to Bristol in 1495 seeking fame as an explorer, and while he did find it – as the discoverer of North America no less – historians have subsequently made a sport of progressively downgrading his so-called achievement. The first shot was an easy one: North America was discovered by hunter-gatherers from Asia *yonks* ago. You can only be surprised that Cabot and the crew of the *Matthew* didn't surmise themselves that they weren't the first to the continent when they *saw other people there*. It must be remembered that the man was desperate to claim the top spot and thus receive a mention in that coveted journal, the *Guinness Book of Records*. So what about first European? Well, sorry Johnny Boy, but what about Leif Ericson and the lads who made the trip at the end of the first millennium? Oh yes, the Vikings went to North America. They wrote about it, had a couple of good-natured rucks with the locals, and even built a settlement in Nova Scotia. They say the Canadian archeologists who uncovered these Norse structures named them, somewhat cruelly, things like 'Bain of Cabot', 'Cabot's Demotion' and so on. Perhaps the erstwhile explorer could still salvage *something* in that he could say that he was the first European to discover America in the *second* millennium, and furthermore that he did it without knowing it was there. This would preserve the hoary image of the *Matthew*'s voyage as one of remarkable bravado and danger; for the tale goes that Cabot and his crew did not know if they would sail off the end of the world once they got past 40°W.

But I'm afraid to say that even this slightly more modest story is a load of rubbish, and whoever believes it has not heard the word on the street in my hometown. I'm sorry to say it (I'm not) but Cabot didn't really achieve anything significant. His part in the age of exploration, which had already become vanishingly small, is about to be eliminated. The fact is there was a group of Bristolians who had been going to North America *years* before Cabot rocked up, and, what's more, he only ended up getting there because they inadvertently let slip the way.

You see, the Bristolian seafarers had been keeping the landmass a secret, for it was mixed up in a little tax scam they had going. Cabot, on the other hand, crowed about his 'discovery' to all who would listen. This is the only reason we remember him and not them. It's loudmouths that make it into the history books, while those who achieve what they achieve under the radar live on only in legend. All John Cabot did was sign his name on something that had already been accomplished. His fame is entirely due to the luck of overhearing a drunken fellow in a Bristol tavern telling his companion of a land far to the west where the natives dress in animal skins, the fish are plentiful, and the wild forest comes down to the shore.

You see, back in the 1400s Bristol fishermen had to pay a terribly high tax on what they called jack, which is our cod. The tax was really a crime, and it made the price of fish intolerably high and bankrupted many honest fishermen. A group of such fishermen, straining under the weight of this unjust levy, got together to try and do something about it. The tax was charged by the Society of Merchant Venturers (in league with the guild) – but having an interest in exploration the secretive conglomerate charged a ship nothing if the purpose of the voyage was to find new lands. And so the plucky fishermen simply started calling their fishing trips 'Great Expeditions'. They would sail off over the horizon and then just go round in circles getting drunk on rum. After a suitable amount of time had elapsed they would return, kissing their teeth and bemoaning the depressing emptiness of the Atlantic Ocean. Of course, the belly of the boat would be full of jack, and the payload would be unloaded secretly into the underground tunnels that run beneath Bristol like so many arteries and veins. Via the catacombs the delicious fish would be secreted off to be sold at this or that market. To this day, cavers report that there are sections of the tunnels that still stink to high heaven of dried fish. It is rumoured that somewhere there is an Eldorado-like unrecovered cache of preserved jack awaiting discovery.

Anyway, the truly surprising part of the story is what follows. These Bristol fisherman started to go further and further in search of bigger catches. They would always make sure to bag a few outlandish creatures such as you find far out to sea. These could be brought home as curios and would allay any fears that their 'explorations' were nothing but a tax-avoidance scheme. The universe, however, thinks it very witty to turn make-believe into reality. And so it was that on one of their fishing trips the fishermen accidently discovered a continent. They called it Hi-Brazil, which is the name of a giant island in the Atlantic spoken of in ancient Celtic mythology.

At this point the fishermen could have easily come back and made a big announcement and fuss about what they had found. Their original crime would have no doubt been buried in the awesomeness of their actual discovery. But they didn't, partly because they had never wanted to be explorers anyway, but also partly because the beautiful bays of Nova Scotia, Maine and Massachusetts were teeming with jack. And so they resolved to keep the discovery a secret and continued smuggling their generous hauls back to Bristol for many more years. Of course, their tongues loosened over time. After all, who could resist sharing such stories for long? For the fishermen had established contact with another world. It is said that they often told tales about the native tribes they encountered: their intriguing hairstyles, their well-run farms, their skill in woodwork and other crafts. The natives' way of life was so pleasing that a few of the seafarers concerned thought of settling out in Hi-Brazil themselves. It is said that the fishermen picked up the native language over the years (most likely an Unami tongue spoken by the Lenni Lanape people) and would often use it as a code back home in Bristol when they wanted to disguise their speech from their fellows. It is even said that many prominent terms in the Bristol dialect are originally Unami words, the most famous instance being 'gert'. All this raises the intriguing spectre of a synchronistic civilisation of east coast First Nation tribes and Bristolians. Unfortunately for all concerned, however, the tax-free wealth that the jack-smuggling scam was netting them kept the fishermen returning home to Bristol. And eventually the tales that the boys could not resist sharing in the taverns were to put an end to the good thing they had going. It is a lesson I have learned myself through bitter experience: watch you don't enjoy the story too much, for the reality has a way of slipping away while you do.

Venetian nobleman Giovanni Caboto had moved to Bristol to reinvent himself as John Cabot, explorer extraordinaire. He was here whipping up excitement and trying to get backing from the Society of Merchant Venturers and other rich folk. Bristol's a relatively easy town to make it in because we're quite an accepting bunch. Nevertheless, it wasn't all plain sailing for little Giovanni. He faced much rejection, but eventually the boy got his break. Picture the scene: he had had a long day and was sat at the bar in the Hatchet. He'd only got a few coins chinking about in his bucket and seeing as they weren't enough to buy a ship, hire a crew, and go-a discovering, he was going to drink them instead. He was plotted up there, morosely glugging on his bitter like a big Italian baby, not minding a jot that his beard was covered in foam, when he heard something from a table behind him that made him suddenly alert. No one else in the bar paid the tale any mind, for they'd all heard it a hundred times before: it was the one about a land far to the

west, where the natives dress in animal skins, the fish are plentiful, and the wild forest comes down to the shore.

The seafarer described how to get there (turn left at
Greenland), including all the tricky currents and so on. Cabot
gratefully jotted this down, downed his pint, and went out
again, redoubling his efforts to find sponsors and get his ship
together. He eventually set sail in the *Matthew* and sometime
later (in 1497 to be exact) landed in North America. The
fishermen had let their secret continent slip from their grasp
and their little scam was up, for Cabot's 'discovery' was going
to change the life of all Bristol seafarers forever. Very soon he
was back and crowing about his great expedition and what
he had found. He was given audience with the king and His
Majesty and the royal court were all most entertained by the
story about a land far to the west, where the natives dress in
animal skins, the fish are plentiful, and the wild forest comes
down to the shore.

Of course, the fishermen's deceptions do not bother us at
all today. Cabot's, when he stole that information and claimed
it as his own, is a little more salacious perhaps. However,
the whole sorry tale of what ended up happening in the
Americas, of what the European presence there led to, of
who benefited and how, and the part that our city played in it
all, is a crime of such magnitude that I simply cannot elaborate it here. It is a truth so true and so heavy that it could sink
a little book such as this.

Tales of Banksy

Over the last few decades we have watched graffiti make a
transition from crime to art. The question of whether graffiti is art is a really dull one, because you'd have to be a total
spoon to argue that it isn't. Of course, these things always

happen quicker in the understanding than they do in the law, and painting on walls without permission is still a crime. This disjuncture has created some strange situations, for graffiti art by a well-known artist can be very valuable indeed, and so landowners and leaseholders are put in the unfamiliar position of having wealth illegally smeared upon their property. Such characters had long been in the habit of scrubbing any graffiti off as quickly as possible, but the vast sums that some of this art is now worth has made them think twice. Property owners and developers are now in the position of having to learn a great deal about graffiti, which was always the artform of choice for criminals, dropouts, radicals and scallywags. This is the reason that Network Rail employees are now required to go on art courses designed to help them identify 'Banksys'.

Outside of the Avon, North Somerset and South Gloucestershire area there is much speculation about the true identity of street artist Banksy, but within those limits I think it is safe to say that most people know his name, even if they do not consider him a personal friend. Back in the day, Julian Stops was in a little crew of graffiti artists who all went to the Barton Hill Youth Club. They called themselves the DryBreadZ Crew, and they owe much to a youth worker called John Nation, for, in recognising their talent, he encouraged the young artists to paint freely on available walls. Julian himself once said that, 'John Nation, that shouty, red-faced little social worker who made it all happen, has had more impact on the shape of British culture over the last twenty years than anyone else to come from this city.'

Naturally, everyone in the Crew gave themselves a cool name. There was Tes, Kator, Lokey, Inky, and many others. Julian chose the moniker 'Robin the Bank', which was later shortened to Banksy. Or at least that's one story, and one that has inevitably been fertile soil for the speculation that Banksy was considering a career as a bank robber or bank teller (or both) before settling down into graffiti art. Julian himself, on the other hand, insists that it is because he played in goal for the Easton Cowboys Football Club, and that the pseudonym comes from the England goalie of yesteryear, Gordon Banks.

Of course, lots of people have tried to piggyback on Banksy's fame into the limelight themselves, or else just make a quick buck. One man set up a stall at a Bristol craft fair selling what he claimed were signed Banksy prints and called the stall, in a brilliant double bluff, 'The Fake Banksy Stall'. If he had called it 'The Banksy Stall', of course no one would have bought it, but his denial planted the seed that this may well be the kind of name that Banksy himself would give his stall, and so the fake prints started to sell like hot cakes. The legend goes that Banksy rushed down there and set up a stall right next door called 'The Real Fake Banksy Stall'.

On slow news days journalists sometimes like to report that Banksy has been arrested and his identity finally uncovered. The method is simple: find any old arrest and say that whoever has been taken in is Banksy. It's an easy article and it always gets plenty of hits. After a particularly convincing one, where the entire world seemed to think that Banksy was indeed the disgraced guru figure, Swami Rishi Philaranandra (real name David Tonyton), the real Banksy decided it would be fun to prove his continuing freedom. Just as the Swami was on trial, Banksy did a prominent new piece down at Bristol harbourside. It was 'The Girl with a Pierced Eardrum'. The media, of course, swarmed to take a look at it to try and judge for themselves whether it was genuine. The public took an interest too, and local residents became so enraged at the lack of parking spaces that they tried to deface the image. A burger van close by took a much more positive view, and quickly invented a Banksy Bacon Bap to capitalise on the new footfall.

My last Banksy slice is something of a challenge. Not to me you understand, but to you. It is said that Banksy and his best friend Inky (real name Shams Bidvideo) did some pieces in Easton back in the day using ultraviolet paint. Of course, they're as invisible as the Clifton Big Cat, but if you get one of those special lights that bar staff use to tell the difference between fivers and tenners then it may be that you could find one of them. Traipsing round Easton in the rain (I swear it rains more in Easton) and shining a light on walls is surely a good investment considering the epic dividends that await you should you find the missing Banksy. I should warn you, however, that it is quite possible that that little scamp Julian Stops made the whole thing up, and that as you pass under the viaduct that runs over Greenbank cemetery, combing the brickwork with your weird little lamp, you will see his cheeky face peering down at you, laughing, laughing, laughing.

The Cycle Path Gang

I first became aware of this story in about 2005 as a simple warning: *do not go onto the cycle path past sunset.* An urban legend is often the shadow of something real, and in the case of this one you would not want to run into the thing itself. For this reason I have always followed the advice. For those who don't know already, 'cycle path' here denotes the Bristol and Bath Railway Path, that ex-train track turned beautiful walk and cycle way that runs from Temple Meads station, over rivers and canals and marshes, through forests, tunnels and defunct stations where ruddy-faced matrons sell ice creams, sodas and cups of tea, past a charming stretch of track where steam trains chortle along (a life-size Thomas the Tank Engine often among them), and brings you out in Bath; all without going up or down a hill. The path is managed by such dignified institutions as the Avon Frome Partnership, South Gloucestershire Council, Bristol City Council, Bath &

North East Somerset Council and Sustrans, and I'm sure that none of the nice people involved foresaw the plethora of despicable uses to which their enlightened project would be put, and as such I have no wish to drag their good names through the mud – particularly seeing as they maintain an admirably mud-free cycleway.

Still, reports started to come in about a violent gang operating on the path. The gang's aim, at least at first, seems to have been theft. These weren't standard muggings, however: the gang was somewhat creative. One of the tactics they used was to crouch down in the bushes holding a wire over the path. When a cyclist came by they would suddenly whip up the wire, taking the victim sharply off of their bike. The bike would then be taken and the prone cyclist attacked and robbed of his wallet and phone.

Now, the gang (who were presumably youths but I only say that because of stereotypes, having no evidence regarding what age they were) was very violent and often beat their victims, or even sliced their flesh with knives. This wouldn't be so unusual if it wasn't for the ritualistic element in these attacks. Someone would be walking home along the path, probably only moments after sunset, feeling like they should walk quickly while there was still some light in the sky, when suddenly out from the shadows would come the gang. They would surround the victim in a ring, and close in on them, all in step with one another.

An ingenious, efficient and original gang of criminals. This was how the story started. And it was a good one. It made my spine tingle deliciously, especially when I found myself on the path near to sunset. Crime is scary stuff and always makes for spicy tales. As time went on the reports slowly started to emphasise the violence over the mugging. The gang would take your stuff, sure, but even after you had given them everything they would not be finished. Gathered in a circle around you they would submit you to trials of pain. The implements they used were said to have became more elaborate, turning from Stanley knives to soldering irons and pliers. It was even said that they started catching people with antique bear-traps.

As the horrors ramped up the financial motive of the crimes began to fade into the background. And then one day my friend Lizzie Fanton told me about a savage encounter her friend's cousin had told her friend about. The cousin was on the path going through Lawrence Hill, and the weak winter sun had just set over the warehouses. He happened to have over £100 on him, plus a quarter of high-quality skunk-weed, but the gang totally ignored the offerings when he presented them in return for his personal safety. They beat him to the ground with the short bits of two by four they brandished and kept beating him as he fell. They were rehearsed: their sticks swishing back and forth through the dusky air in absolute synchronisation. The beating accomplished, the gang removed the cousin's right shoe and proceeded to pull the toenail from his big toe. He screamed and pleaded while they worked in utter silence.

The normal, rational motivation of personal enrichment now sets on this story and something terrible rises into the void that is left. The gang had always been unidentifiable: at the beginning it was because they used hoodies to shroud their faces in shadow. But then I started to hear reports of the masks. It was said that as they circled their victim they would be chanting something. It was not simply a repeated phrase either, but something long and complicated in an ancient tongue, full of sharp Xs and Chs, and guttural consonants cut straight from the larynx. The purposes behind the attacks had become darkly religious. The gang members were no longer climbing the ordinary criminal career ladder. They had given themselves over to their activity, moving through the criminal and into the cultic. They attacked not for money, or power, or even pleasure: but as an act of worship. Violence had become a god to whom they were exquisitely obedient. Violence has its own dreams and wishes, and for the most part they are (thankfully) repressed and kept locked in the imaginary hinterland of the forbidden. The cycle path gang opened the channel, and thus was naked Violence herself able to step forward into the dirty light of reality.

The gang's activity seemed to die down somewhat from around 2011. You still hear about them sometimes though. A woman called Chelsea Jen told me she saw them in the distance, one dusk in the summer of 2015. They were drawing around someone, emerging from behind walls and trees. The victim was terrified, meeting masked faces each way that she turned. Chelsea was somewhere between Staple Hill and Mangotsfield. On one side there was an abandoned house, with the windows and doors boarded up, and on the other was a little copse. Beyond that lay a desolate field. Soon the gang was circling the victim, who appeared to be talking and gesticulating a great deal. They were stepping around her in a kind of formation. Their movement was beautiful, the choreography faultless. Each right leg would dart out to the side and each left would follow in a graceful arc, the toe scraping lightly across the ground. In this undulating rhythm the gang circled their victim, who had sunk to the floor. Chelsea slowed but kept walking. Fascination tussled with terror, and bravery and concern shouted their pieces over the top. As she approached she moved into the trees to avoid the orange pillars of light beneath the street lamps. The gang all wore plimsoles and their feet on the gravelly path made no sound. Chelsea was now close enough to hear the victim ask something that might have been, 'Say what?' but the poor thing was so choked up with tears that it was hard to tell. She looked to be in her forties. She knelt on the ground with a shopping bag by her side. Her shoulders drooped in resignation. The gang was dressed all in black. Their masks were white, but covered in patterns of various kinds. Chelsea was transfixed. And then, though she was well hidden in the trees, one of the gang stopped dancing and turned so that the black holes of its mask pointed directly toward her. *I can't be visible!* thought Chelsea, knowing herself to be well in the darkness of the trees. A scream ripped through the air. It went out over the dark field and then drew back into silence. Chelsea's body snapped into action and she ran. She pounded the cycle path beneath her, took the first exit from it, and did not stop running until she had reached home.

SLENDER MAN

I **WANT TO SAY** before I begin that this really is the scariest story in the whole collection. Some of the others are somewhat spooky, or a bit sinister, but this is the only one that creeped me out to such an extent that I wanted to stop finding out about it. When I heard it first, from a child in Bristol Children's Hospital, I was excited. I felt I had hit the jackpot. I will call the boy Solomon, although as with everybody who spoke to me I have changed his name to protect his identity. Of course, I was very grateful Solomon had given me such a spooky story for my collection and I thanked him profusely. 'Great story!' said I.

Solomon's face was waxy and expressionless. His eyes clouded over. The nurses had upped his dosage. He seemed to be sinking back into his mountain of pillows. And yet he was perfectly lucid when he spoke. His voice was small but very serious: 'People think it's a story. But it's not. It's true.' I lowered my head in shame. I had treated what he had told me as mere entertainment, when in fact he had been sharing an encounter with someone or some*thing* that he believes to pose a genuine danger to him and his peers.

I can be forgiven perhaps, for at that stage I did not know where the story was yet to take me. Countless children would tell me earnestly about the same complex of issues: mysterious disappearances, prophetic nightmares, hideous screams in the woods, and all of it something to do with this so-called 'Slender Man'. Sure, there were discrepancies and conflicting accounts, but is this reason enough to ignore such a mountain of testimony? Without fail the adult world refuses to believe children when it comes to such topics. We silence them with cuddles or scolding, or some manipulative mixture of the two. Even when there has been yet another disappearance, and little Mary's knot of best friends insist her obsession with the Slender Man is somehow relevant to the investigation, their witness is unilaterally dismissed without a second thought. The police hang up and list the call as a prank.

I doubt a child would ask the following rhetorical question, and so it remains for me to do so. How many children have to go missing before society heeds what the playground has known for years? *The Slender Man is real.*

* * *

A long time ago there was a family that nobody liked. They were nasty and scary. They fought and they bullied. Their community rejected them. The more they were hated the more hateful they became. The more abuse they received, the more they seemed capable of giving, especially to each other. They moved to a tiny house in the woods with a white picket fence and a bright green door. People forgot about them.

* * *

These days it is considered best practice to give a TRIGGER WARNING at the top of a story or talk in order to signal content that people may find upsetting. Of course, us storytellers have used Trigger Warnings for thousands of years, knowing full well that if one's aim is to terrify and appal the audience, earnestly warning them of your intentions first is a jolly good start. A potent form of Trigger Warning that you may have encountered is the author literally begging you to stop reading or listening. A famous Slender Man video, for instance, is entitled simply 'DO NOT WATCH'. The video in question is generally regarded a fake. However, I suspect that the reason for the cautionary title is not, in this case, there to accentuate suspense or play a simple trick of reverse psychology. It is well known among children that the Slender Man stalks those who find out most about him. It is these children who end up finding alien thoughts and commands appearing in their minds. I suspect the title of the video came late in post-production, after the dreams had started. Probably the children who made the video didn't even want to post it in the end but found themselves compelled to by an irresistible force. Perhaps they had saved just enough conscious control to change the title before it was uploaded.

Of course, everyone starts by not believing in Slender Man, and folk commonly watch these videos only to prove their bravery, or from simple curiosity. However, a kind of fascination soon takes hold, and one finds oneself clicking on the next link, and the next, and the next. Over the following days and nights you get into the stories, and read nothing else. Then at a certain point (for me it came while I was browsing a voluminous Slender Man image-thread) there is a kind of jolt where you are genuinely spooked for the first time. It is soon after this that the dreams begin.

Thus, even by reading this story you could be endangering yourself. Of course, the danger could merely be psychological. It could just be that Slender Man is the sort of cancerous meme that, once having entered the human brain, somehow survives beyond what would be usually expected of childish prattle and online follies. Perhaps Slender Man is a special kind of story, one that 'stays with you'. There are certainly many stories that do this, that wait somewhere in the mind, silently generating terror. There are stories that it is better not to hear, just as there are things that it is better not to see. This is what the psychologists working on the murder investigation concluded, after those two young girls in the USA were found to have repeatedly stabbed their school friend in the woods. The story of the Slender Man was at the heart of the matter, of course. They said they did it 'for' Slender Man; that the victim was a gift for him. But – and the psychologists working on the case insisted on this – Slender Man *himself* wasn't involved. 'Slender Man is not real,' they said: he is every bit as make-believe as Mario or Luigi. It is just that in this instance, the psychologists explained, the fictional character managed to convince two otherwise normal children to murder their friend.

And I do believe that this thesis can tolerably explain the whole Slender Man phenomenon. But anyway, whether the Slender Man be fiction or phantom or something far more corporeal, I must warn you – and I am being most serious here, considering that this story involves real blood and genuine loss – that you read on at your own risk.

✳ ✳ ✳

The council never knew about the house in the woods. Social workers never called. Some say that the family, despite being pariahs, had some kind of contact or benefactor high up in City Hall. The Lord Mayor himself was said to be seen leaving late one sticky summer's eve. Some of the really outlandish gossip had it that the family were actually entangled in some kind of secret experiment: one involving American agents in sunglasses and the like. Anyway, whether it was by incompetence, weariness or design, Bristol City Council and the other powers-that-be did not bother the family in the woods. They lived there in a little red-brick cottage that looked like a Sylvanian Families' doll's house and were uniquely miserable. Do you know what distinguishes a monster from a beast? There are many instances of each type of beast. The Bristol crocodile is a beast, for instance, for there are many crocodiles in the world. Monsters, on the other hand, are exceptional: there is only one of each monster. A bad family is a kind of beast, and a particularly tricky one to deal with at that. But as beastly as this family was, they still weren't so very out of the ordinary. After all, every family is a bit beastly from time to time, and the difference here was merely one of degree. I'm not defending them. From what I hear they did some very horrible things indeed. I'm just saying that these horrible things were like lots of other horrible things that you may have heard about. However, what they created was a monster. You couldn't call him anything else. The Slender Man was born, or at least this is what many of the children in the North Somerset, Avon and South Gloucestershire areas hold, the day that he murdered his family.

* * *

If you think about it from Slender Man's perspective, only appearing to those who have read lots about him, or who spend a lot of time combing over supposed photographs of him on the Internet, is the perfect cover. For when the police investigate Little Jonny's disappearance and find that he has been obsessed with Slender Man (perhaps this very book rests by his bedside) then, of course, everything is explained to them. Poor Jonny is the latest victim of brainwashing. Vile forums like Something Awful or 4chan, toxic Twitter feeds, banned videos and such are all destroying the minds of impressionable children. It was the same with the Video Nasties of the 1980s. The police will shake their heads. The child will be described as vulnerable. The parents will be vilified. Mothers at coffee mornings will ask why Jonny's parents ever let the boy use the Internet unmonitored. Perhaps the pity for Jonny himself will ferment, and soon the papers will present him as utterly contemptible and uniquely danger-ous. Across the nation, individuals will theatrically bolt their doors and make a great show of never letting their own chil-dren out of sight. Their own Little Molly Moo is safe and thus 'good', while Jonny has dirtied himself with the unsafe Internet and is now 'bad'. It is bad form to grieve the bad, and even worse to waste resources helping them. And thus the search parties will never reach the deepest part of the woods, and little Jonny will never be saved. Slender Man really is rather clever like that.

* * *

Solomon's story began when he heard of a strange man who local kids had been seeing in the woods. They lived out past Kingswood at the beginning of the Cotswolds. The man apparently always carried a shotgun with him. The more sceptical among the kids said it was just a farmer. But then why was he wearing a very dapper black suit? Solomon described him as tall and slim, though beyond that he said he would say very little. Hundreds of children have described him to me, but they can never say anything satisfactory about the face, except that he is as white as cartridge paper. In the playground Solomon had heard the rumours flying around. They said that Slender Man lived in a house in the woods. They said that the shotgun he carried was the one he had used to kill his family. But then they also said he worked for a secretive government agency, kidnapping children for use in the bizarre rituals and the blood-cults that proliferate among the powerful. There was talk of aliens and tentacles. Silly talk, concluded Solomon and his friends. They knew the stories were untrue. But what was the truth in that case? The braver among them (who together formed a clique of which Solomon was the rightful chief) decided to go into the woods and do some investigating. They set out one day after school.

* * *

The Internet allows rumours to proliferate. We all know this. At first people would take some joy in detailing Slender

Man's gruesome exploits. He pinned people to trees with one hand (thin and bony but unnaturally strong) and then ripped open their bellies and pulled out their guts with the other. As time went on the mythology changed somewhat. Slender Man's preferred tactic became to stalk children until they went mad. He drove them crazy with terror until they willingly joined him in his woodland home. One child I met during the research period, who lives in Failand on the edge of Bristol's notorious Leigh Woods, told me that Slender Man does what he does only to provide play friends for his murdered son.

A 14-year-old girl who I will call Elle, who lived for a while in a foster home just the other side of the bridge in Clifton, gave me an account that seemed to extend the Slender Man's fatherliness. Elle told me that actually, far from hurting children, Slender Man takes in runaways and protects them. She told me that the little house is as big as a mansion inside. She also said that Slender Man can help you avenge yourself on adults who have done you wrong. On the Internet one will find legions of young people begging Slender Man to come to their aid.

Solomon and his friends really went about their expedition in an exemplary way. By triangulating the sightings reported by their peers they had figured that there was an area of some 5 hectares or so, just a few miles east of Hanham, where the figure was likely to reside. They found the house about an hour before dusk. The sky was bright but the earth was dark. There was a fire flickering inside and smoke was rising from the chimney.

* * *

In the months of research that followed my chat with Solomon, I often became incredulous at the point where children described Slender Man's house. For they would often describe exactly the same house as Solomon had told me about. The description had seemed so quaint that it could only be total fantasy. Furthermore, they would describe it in different locations. Initially I believed that I had understood what had happened: the folks of one part of Bristol had built an urban legend around a strange little house and the story had spread. Though the story changed as it moved across the city, the description of the house was somehow left untouched by the process of Chinese whispers. Did you know that tornados can sometimes pick something up, like a baby in a bathtub say, and, while they smash everything else to bits, carry this one item safely and plonk it down softly some miles away? Stories can do the same thing.

Solomon and his companions had approached the house with great caution. Getting down low they had snuck up to the door, keeping below the sight of anyone who might be watching from behind the net curtains. Once they were at the door they knocked hard and then retreated behind a large oak that stood on the edge of the clearing. They crouched and watched the cottage intently, ready to explode into a run at a moment's notice. But there was no sign of movement from the strange little place. The fire flickered; creating shadows that for a moment looked like a person standing and watching, but were only shadows.

Eventually they started discussing their next move and, as they did so, they turned around and sat down with their back against the tree. It was then they saw him. He had been standing some way behind them in the woods, watching them watching his house.

I picture them not so much running from the clearing as plummeting from it, moving back toward town the way meteorites plummet toward the earth.

But once they got home and reflected on their situation they were disappointed in themselves. They had not got a decent look at the figure who had been watching them. They could have said something to him. They decided to go back the next day, but this time with the protection of someone's older brother, who was nearly 18 years old. They found their way back to the clearing all right. At first they thought it couldn't be the same one, but it was the place, for sure. Only the cottage was gone. Naturally the older brother was displeased to have been drawn into a childish round of make-believe and clipped his sibling round the earhole.

＊ ＊ ＊

After this Solomon's friends had been happy to forget about it. He himself had struggled, however. He dreamed of Slender Man. In his dreams Slender Man got closer and closer, although Solomon still never got a good look at him. Some say that to look at Slender Man, to see his face, is to surrender control over one's own actions.

Solomon is a scrupulously good person. He is a dutiful son and a reliable friend. He works hard at school and is a promising footballer. He is courteous. While he forgives others fairly easily, any minor infraction of his own is like a stain to him. So imagine his horror, then, as he became aware of a strong sense that Slender Man was demanding something of him. Slender Man wanted him to 'do things'. Just to cognise the specific acts asked of him was agony, as were the waves of compulsion the poor boy felt to carry them out, to bring them from mere notion to horrible reality. The doctors say that Solomon is fighting his illness bravely, let's hope he continues to fight his urges with the same determination.

＊ ＊ ＊

I spoke to more of Bristol's children, but didn't again meet a child who claimed to have encountered the Slender Man. At least not one I believed. I felt eager to drop the story by that point. I myself had started to have dreams that featured Slender Man. There was one more thing I wanted to do before finishing my research though. Elle had told me where to find Slender Man's cottage in Leigh Woods and I wanted to follow her directions, just to see. I've tried to communicate to you here some of the terror associated with Slender Man because that is my job. I am a storyteller after all. But while I may have a somewhat overactive imagination, at the end of the day I am aware that the story is very unlikely to have any truth in it. Which explains why I felt more than a bit silly when I went out to Leigh Woods. But imagine how humbled I was when Elle's somewhat cryptic instructions *actually led me to a little red-brick cottage!* The windows were painted gaily in yellow and it had a bright green door, just like Solomon had described. It had a tiled roof and was surrounded by a little picket fence. It looked like the third little pig's house. There was a light on inside and smoke was rising from the chimney. I walked once around the place, dumbstruck with surprise. Actually, if you think about it, it is not all that surprising that this odd little house in the woods exerts a certain fascination over children. Probably it is a wood keeper's cottage, or perhaps home to a deliciously eccentric old lady. Maybe she would offer me tea and a thick slice of malt loaf and butter. I very nearly knocked. But then standing before the green door I suddenly felt very self-conscious. Journalists knock on doors but traditionally storytellers wait to be invited. I could see nothing moving behind the net curtains. My breath was floating in the cool forest air and the light was beginning to fade. I am not quite sure why I started running, or why I couldn't seem to stop. I did not look behind me until I was over the bridge, returned to the relative safety of Bristol town.

BRISTOL FREE STATE

FREEDOM IS A difficult thing to define and an even more difficult thing to achieve. We can know it by its opposite perhaps, which is slavery. Bristol's Scipio Africanus was a slave. He may have been happy-go-lucky, or so the legend goes, but he was enslaved. It doesn't matter how many cherubs you put on his tombstone: the guy was not a free man.

Or then, perhaps he was. I mean, if he was really happy, in his soul, as they say he was – then perhaps he *was* free. Perhaps that *is* freedom. It depends on how you define it. You do hear about some people who cannot be caged: those whom the prison never gets inside, even while they are inside the prison. They have a smile on their faces, and their defiance is an un-cauterisable wound that no authority can heal. It is said that such spirits cannot be robbed of their ability to walk through the open door of happiness, and as such they are always free.

But Scipio *couldn't* just walk out the door, could he? Maybe the magical happiness door was open, the one covered in rainbows and unicorns, but not the real door. He couldn't do as he chose.

Surely freedom is simply more choice? Actually, no. 'Freedom of choice' is merely the freedom a supermarket grants you. It's nice enough, but it is not the freedom you have a revolution for, is it? When you stand upon the bar-ricade waving the blood-red flag, it is for something grander than a wide selection of gluten-free cakes and confectionary. Rather, it is for some great change in society: one that you hope will free the people from their bondage.

Are people even in bondage today? Many of the people in the following stories would argue so. People, so far as I can tell, are almost always wrapped up in one kind of bondage or another. Leaving aside for the moment the fact that there are still *actual slaves* in our society, consider the situations of bond-age that poverty has the power to create. And then there is the spiritual bondage of capitalism itself: we're all of us enslaved to the logic of the market, duty-bound to mould our lives to its will. Anyone who opposes it is being unrealistic. The dream world of Capital has assumed the mantle of reality, and everything else is relegated to mere opinion. You can be who-ever you want, so long as you serve Mammon the destructive money God in body and deed, even if not in word.

And I'm sure you'll agree that some equivalent bondage can be found in every era of human life, at least since we fell into civilisation. I mean, feudalism was no better was it? So has the human race *never* been free? What is freedom anyway? I don't have the answers: all I have is these tales about the Bristolians who thought they did.

Ashton Court Festival vs. the Iron Lady

Maybe freedom is just having a good time. Many, many people in Bristol define it this way. The worldview of some of these people is admirable in its simplicity. It goes like this: 'The Man' wants you to work a boring 9–5 job, have a boring, hetero-normative family and generally be a pro-ductive citizen. Freedom consists in not doing these things, and instead having an outrageously, stupidly good time. Like all worldviews, it explains some situations better than others. One it describes very well indeed is the epic saga of Ashton Court Festival.

Thatcher came into power the same year that the Ashton Court Festival began, so the story goes, and Ashton Court can be viewed as a kind of rebellion against Thatcherism. Thatcher is as much of an urban legend in Bristol as she is around the rest of the isles (for example it is said she was the only ever female member of the Society of Merchant Venturers). In this story, the Iron Lady gives her dominion two clear choices:

monetize your existence and align your values with the logic of the market, or face brutal police violence. Thus, to be at an early Ashton Court Festival, with no fence, no tickets, no wages, no fees, and no profit for anyone, watching Bristol's legendary Moonflowers playing naked on the stage, with fifty naked hippy kids swirling and swaying about up there with them, was to witness a form of rebellion. The Moonflowers' whole lives were devoted precisely to *not* being productive citizens. And Ashton Court was the grand climax of a full year's glorious unproductiveness. 'Take drugs and duck' was one of the band's well-known slogans. I'm not quite sure what it means actually, and I'm not entirely certain they did either.

What a lot of people don't know, least of all the Moonflowers, is that all that unproductiveness took a great deal of organisation. At the centre of Ashton Court Festival there was a formidable maelstrom of administrative activity, and in the centre of that there was a remarkable bloke called Royce Creasy. Royce was a biker and an F1 pit mechanic. He had been inspired by a Hell's Angels festival to set up a shin-dig in his native Bristol. Admittedly, the biker gathering had been a quite simple affair, with the main draw being the fairly niche activity of standing in a field and taking turns hitting each other with planks of wood. But Royce was sure that with a few adjustments the set-up could work for other folks. The guy was a perfect storm of libertarian, tough-as-nails, no-bullshit biker values, and the ruthless organisational skills that you hone as part of an elite F1 pit team.

He chose the spot well. It fell between the borders of two police authorities, a no man's land between Bristol and North Somerset, with neither force really wanting to address the issue for many years, buying the festival precious time. Originally Royce was working with a few hippies from New Zealand, but they were way too laid back to deal with the formidable horsepower of his personality. A few heads from

Bristol filled the gap, and the crew ran the festival on and off for thirty years, fighting for much of this time against closure by the authorities. The establishment's growing determination to scupper the proceedings does make one wonder whether The Man really does have a nefarious investment in us living humdrum lives. Eventually the pressure against the festival was constant. It was as if Ashton Court was happening deep under the sea, with the system relentlessly pushing in on the festival, searching for any little crack which would give it an excuse to start pissing on the parade.

There were years of victory and years of defeat, of course, but the story of Ashton Court is one of slow decline really. The enemy took many forms, but rest assured that it was Mammon the money God behind it all. The insult to her – the free availability of love and happiness – was a scandal that she could not abide. Bristol constabulary wanted the festival to pay £50,000 to have the event policed. The force would have known that this was a product that the hippies did not want, priced at a rate they could not afford. Health and Safety gone mad needed constant money: fire-retardant bollards, obligatory training days about how to never climb trees, mandatory resuscitation equipment for all bassists; the list of requirements went on and on. There were fees you had to pay to companies you never knew existed to fix problems that didn't exist.

So 'They' won in the end, and the gathering no longer takes place today. Still, it was fun while it lasted. And, much to everyone's delight, the Ashton Court Free Festival outlasted Thatcher's long-ass reign by many happy summers.

Bluesies

Bristol, surely more than any other place in the land, lives for parties, gatherings, shindigs, dos, raves, blow-outs and the like. Perhaps we're flattering ourselves by labelling such experiences rebellions. But then again, perhaps rebellion *should* feel this good. Anyway, even if you aren't trying to have a rebellion, and are just throwing a regular party, there is always the danger that the powers that be will interpret your event as an insurrection regardless.

Bluesies are the legendary 'speakeasies' of the Jamaican community in Bristol. Basically, they were unlicensed bars. I did a whole lot of digging on this topic, and thoroughly enjoyable it was, too. The thing is though, there just isn't that much to report. You want a story to have some mystery and suspense to it, but you know all I ever found in a Bluesy? A nice time. The atmosphere is really nice. The music is great. Personally, I don't play dominoes because I'm scared of numbers, but there's that if you want it. People dance and the Wray and Nephews flows. It's not some big secret, 'There ain't nothing going on,' said an old Jamaican fellow to me one evening, 'iss jus people want to have a good time, you know?'

I *do* know. Bluesies are not even really illegal. It's just basically a private party in someone's basement or wherever. You pay for your drinks but that's only to cover the cost. People don't make any profit from it. It's not about that. If you're thinking Bluesies must be a nuisance to neighbours, you're wrong. Bluesies get very few complaints because it is standard practice to invite the neighbours to join in the good time. And once they've been down there they end up loving it the same as anyone would.

So, the reason the police were for so many years intent on breaking them up is something of a mystery. Maybe the

Bohemian theorists are right. Perhaps there is some secret cabal of conspirators who control the establishment and who really just can't stand people having fun. Perhaps *They* are powering some great infernal machine with our dissatisfaction, and the streams of rainbow joy that issue out of Bluesies are a kind of pollutant in their fuel. Or maybe drudgery makes us more amenable to mind-control experiments. Maybe. But then again, perhaps the police were unfairly targeting the Jamaican community for years for absolutely no good reason, continually arresting and harassing them for things white people can do with impunity.

The Mild Mild West

One day the famous stencil artist Banksy, who is – despite what most people seem to think – a woman called Fran Bigalow, was going to do a stencil piece up on the side of a building on Stokes Croft. The piece was going to be a bit of her trademark satirical anti-consumerism. Some rats in a beauty spa or something. There happened to be a guy passing and Banksy, needing someone to spot the ladder while she worked, asked for some help. The two carried on a jovial little chat while the artist got her stuff ready. Well, the fella, who was an old head by the name of Boysie Devan, told Banksy about a legendary 'freeparty' he had been at up on Winterstoke Road. It had come at the end of the rave era, when the police were under orders – direct from Maggie no less – to close the whole scene down, using any means possible. The police had been having an easy time of it because ravers make particularly soft targets for old PC Truncheon. The partygoers would seldom know the police were coming until after they were in a prison cell with lumps on their heads. They were more likely to hug an officer than resist arrest.

The ebullient wave of drugs and music we know as 'rave' is credited, quite correctly, with taming the football hooligans: they got loved-up and joined the cuddle-puddle. For those involved at the time it seemed inevitable that rave culture would soon take the whole world up in a great tide of dopamine and deposit them on the shore of a new land, where Love would finally rule the day. It was beliefs like these that made the poor dudes such super easy targets for the cops. They were, in their own terminology, *fluffy*. Meanwhile, police in Thatcher's Britain were decidedly spiky. It cannot have been pretty seeing a police raid on a Bristol freeparty in this era: fish and barrels come to mind.

But then, after a few very disastrous thrashings, where arms were broken, people were arrested and sound systems were confiscated, something surprising started to happen: the fluffy people fought back. According to Boysie, Winterstoke Road was the rave where the ravers just couldn't take it any more. Dressed in nothing but furry pink boots and fluorescent body paint, armed with nothing but lengths of two-by-four and fire poi, they met the police upon the blasted battleground of Gore's Marsh. Of course, they lost horribly. But their fight was spirited and the story is now immortalised in a famous artwork. For Banksy enjoyed Boysie's yarn so much that she decided right then and there to change what she was painting. That's why the 'Mild Mild West' piece looks different from other Banksys: it was painted on the spur of the moment without using a stencil.

The hideous symbolic end to the rave scene is said to have occurred on Castle Morton common about 50 miles north of here, but, seeing as it was populated by the same Bristol heads as you would have seen at a party in, say, an abandoned warehouse on Feeder Road, then it certainly warrants inclusion here. Before I begin I would like to note that while most of these urban legends have come to me in a very confused state, this one was a particular mess. Each person seemed to tell me an entirely different story about what actually went on. Now, this could, of course, be due to the confused state which attending these events tends to put one. But also, I suspect that for people who put serious time into the rave scene, the parties they attended do have a tendency to get in a bit of a muddle. So it could be that my interlocutors and I have merged many disparate parties into one here. No matter, let's enjoy the legend as it comes down to us.

We should set the scene before we begin. By all accounts rave had been a touchingly peaceful subculture to begin with. The ravers had become heedless of what had been, only a few short years before, the insurmountable boundaries of race, class and sexuality. Strangers were declaring their love for each other in baby voice, giving each other cute presents and long hugs, sharing peak mystical experiences on the dance floor. Once hardened bullies became as religious and sensitive as cows. The rave was a place where runaways and stray souls found their home.

And then there were the glorious individuals who were mixed up in it all. I was told about countless outrageous and unlikely heroes, but we will have to be content with just having a look at one of them. Aide was not, technically speaking, a Bristolian. He had come over from Ireland. He had been on his way to London but had got distracted. Easily done. He always demanded everybody's presence at every party, and showed more commitment to the dancing, frivolity and flowing wine than could have been expected from Bacchus himself. He was generous and flawed and frail and strong, and he was loved. He didn't care about worldly possessions; he was not proud or egotistical; Aide was free. He had danced his way to freedom and he helped many others do the same.

Another asset the Bristol ravers had was a formidable array of tactics for evading the long arm of the law. They had for years been beating Maggie's militarised coppers in an epic game of cat and mouse. Their system of notification was incredibly complicated. These days all you need to do to encrypt a message is download an app, but back in the day in order to get ravers to the rave *sans police*, the sound systems folk who threw the parties had to send out multiple sets of directions, one being the real one and the rest decoys. Only those with the code knew the difference. Of course, there were no mobiles, and these directions were procured by calling various numbers and listening to recorded messages. One of the messages would be the correct one, and you had to know the code to sift it from the many dummies. A man who called himself 'Red Dave' told me, quite sincerely, that the only way to sort the real directions from the false was to be high on LSD. If this is true it is quite funny, because even on those occasions when the coppers did manage to shut the party down with their ultraviolence, the ravers at least had the satisfaction of knowing that somewhere some poor officer of the law was shivering in a corner, oppressed by a fantasia of marching truncheons.

I heard many stories about use of the underground tunnels to arrive at secret locations. A regular meeting place was The Rose of Denmark down at the entrance to the harbour. There is apparently an access point to the catacombs from there, from inside the Ladies' facilities, no less. Lord knows what the regular patrons thought, with droves of scantily clad neon bumblebees and the like disappearing into the loo never to re-emerge.

Many a rave was a drive away, and the only way to get there would be to follow one of the organiser's cars. And you'd better make sure that it wasn't a decoy. One of my informants, I'll call her Hannah, explained to me how delightful it was to be driving one of the dummy cars. You would drive merrily off into Somerset or Gloucestershire and just make whatever left and rights took your fancy. The motley collection of undercover police on your tail would get more and more perplexed and frustrated as you wound them all into a tight knot in the deepest countryside. Then you would stop, by the banks of a sludgy drainage canal perhaps, and everyone would get out. There the undercover lot would be, looking most uncomfortable in their white gloves, spiked blue hair and sparkly hotpants. Then you would simply sit in a muddy field and enjoy a variety of perfectly legal pursuits. Perhaps you would invite people to play 'eye spy', or to find a partner and enjoy a game of 'pat-a-cake'. The poor police officers' faces would go from bemused to enraged as they realised that the pesky ravers had foxed them again. Of course, they would pull their badges out and make a great show of searching you, but you would be clean as a whistle. There was at that time no law against dressing up like an orgiastic space clown and driving into the middle of nowhere.

But by the time of Castle Morton, however, Mammon was clawing her way into the nursery and things were turning seedy as big-time gangsters began taking over the rave scene and introducing their Thatcherite business policies. The money involved in the drug trade was poisoning everything, as was the actual poison that was being used to pad out the drugs themselves. I've heard stories about broken glass being sprinkled onto skunk weed, simultaneously making it weigh more and increasing the seeming potency of the stuff by glittering like (so I'm told) crystals of THC do. What had been a celebration of life and hope was becoming another opportunity for profit, and a testing ground for oppression and violence. A dart dipped in potent capitalism had been shot into the middle of that glorious mass of heaving, sweaty bodies, and darkness was now growing among them.

Worst of all, the police had been locating the raves with increasing success and smashing them with increasing severity.

The ravers were not at all unified about how to counter this trend, or about whether or not they should fight back when it happened. It all seemed to be falling apart. Many key figures had started to flag a little. The shakes, the jitters, and the imaginary friends were not at all uncommon. Aide, a man of indestructibly good temper and an inexhaustible will to keep partying, had got very sick. He had cancer and had been undergoing chemo. He had carried on raving all through this grueling process, however, as indefatigable and cheerful as ever. He was even planning to come to Castle Morton, so perhaps there was still hope yet.

The party started well. They were a long way from anywhere and were not likely to get many complaints. It was up on a beautiful bit of common land. The reason the Bristol sound systems had gone there is some New Age Traveller types were having a quiet little gathering, after having been kicked out of Gloucestershire. There was a convoy of buses and wagons and the like and they were going up on the common to play some acoustic music and have a campfire. Unfortunately for them, the Bristol ravers got wind of this and decided to go up and help the gathering go off with a bang. So, the little family of live-in vehicles was swarmed by space cadets; sound systems popped up like Stonehenges here and there across the common, and the thrum of acid techno had soon spread across the whole environs.

Everyone was there. It was huge. It was the biggest illegal rave the country has ever seen. Aide was there in his hospital gowns and with his drip in tow. How did he get up on top of that truck? It was old skool. They were having it large. The problem was that they had turned up the bass so loud that they did not hear the helicopters when they came in. The police had planned the operation down to the last can of mace. On the edge of the party, furthest from the music, in the kind of 'chillout zone' that always forms where there are comfortable places to pile on top of one another, the police lined up in formation, all in riot gear, and began banging their shields. Of course, you must understand that the testimony of a raver usually comes with something of a tropical twist, but what I've been told is that the coppers looked for all the world like a tribe of demonic Viking warriors. Their eyes rolled around in their heads as they whipped themselves into a battle frenzy. The ravers started to panic: some ran away, some ran around, some hurriedly finished what narcotics they had left, some brought the alarm to the rest of the party, and a few began to arm themselves. A phalanx of the bravest of them faced the police. They held burning sticks from the fire. There was a stand-off. But the police just kept banging their shields and never made their charge, for it was all just a distraction. You see, meanwhile a whole other unit was attacking the sound system directly. They smashed every amp, destroyed every speaker, pulverised the turntables and then started on the records themselves. The DJ, seeing her collection facing destruction, reached out to stop them. Her wrist and several fingers were smashed in a flurry of blows.

In some versions of the story there were police in the trees, dangling from helicopters, even in a tank borrowed from the military. What all those who were present agree upon is that while the clothes and general accoutrements would last many years longer, and though freeparties themselves will likely be around forever, Castle Morton was the night that they dealt the death blow to the scene as it once was. From that moment on it became clear to those in the know that rave culture was never going to reach the heights it had set itself upon. It was beaten down into the mud of the common that night, along with a multitude of glowsticks, tobacco pouches and fluorescent baby's dummies with smiley faces on them.

Just a few short years later, back in Bristol, there was a funeral. It was a de facto ceremony for the passing of the scene, but also for a very special human being. Aide had died. According to his wishes he was to be buried in his adoptive home, Bristol. His family came over from Ireland, of course, and they brought with them the family priest. He asked Aide's friends to say some words about what the departed meant to them and encouraged them to choose some music in his honour. I like picturing the stillness of the cleric and the family as the beat pulsed the walls of the little chapel. I like imagining the way the hook echoed out across the damp cemetery. Perhaps the odd great aunt couldn't resist tapping her toes and nodding her head. The ravers, of course, in their full regalia, partied like it was 1991.

The St Paul's Riots

Another famous stand-off with the authorities was the St Paul's riots of the 1970s. The decade's unemployment had severely affected both the Caribbean communities and the white working-class of Bristol. The National Front had campaigned hard in local and national elections and race relations had deteriorated.

The police had been increasingly targeting young black youths for stop and search. At the same time, they had been ignoring the attacks that many people of colour faced from the increasingly empowered white nationalist elements of society. Paul Stephenson warned Bristol repeatedly of the danger of riots. He was not heeded.

What set them off was some incident with the police raiding the Black and White Café on Grosvenor Road in St Paul's. There are many conflicting accounts but it seems that the police either confiscated alcohol (the café was not licenced and was operating as something of a 'Bluesy' with lock-ins and such) and/or ripped the trousers of a patron of the café during a stop and search. Whatever it was, the incident sparked rioting by around 200 black and white youths who were angered by police abuses of power. Now, some describe the events as merely a display of rage on the part of some underprivileged and downtrodden young men, others see them as a more conscious demonstration of specific discontents. To return to our central theme, I suggest that either of these can be interpreted as an expression of freedom, in that they are both refusals to just lie down and take it. However, whether the riots were political or opportunistic, or some mixture of the two, there is a legend that they had a very surprising and fortuitous unintended consequence.

It is said that the chief of Bristol Police at the time, Chief Donald Waldo, sought out an audience with a popular leader among the rioters. Chief Waldo was worried that the rioting would spread. The police were being pushed back and the disturbance was moving steadily south toward the shopping precinct of Broadmead, where it could do the most damage. Perhaps the Chief was worried of a replay of the weeks of riots in 1832, where the mob eventually reached all the way to Queen's Square and burned the Lord Mayor's house to the ground. And so Waldo was ready to negotiate. If the rioters pulled back, and spared Broadmead, then the police would enter into a new covenant with the neighbourhood of St Paul's. No more raids on Bluesies and other 'illegal' gatherings. So long as they were peaceful, the police would not come and break them up. In return for this, the riot must stop before it spread south into the city. Now, I know this story credits a mob with slightly more ability to make rational decisions than is usually attributed to them, but if you will not ascribe them the agency here then it is beholden on you to explain what else stopped the riot after just a handful of short hours? There was certainly much more anger to go around, and the temptation to loot the shopping precinct for the poor youth involved must have been pretty great. Riots like that usually go on for days. Furthermore, the rioters had overpowered the police. There is that famous quote from an officer on the front line: 'We should be advancing not retreating!' So what stopped the riot? The tale goes that the rioters took the police up on Waldo's offer. And, in the years that followed, the police kept their side of the bargain, and the new covenant was to bear some significant fruit. The new lease of life that St Paul's had, with Bluesies and other gatherings untroubled by police raids, resulted directly in the creation of the so-called 'Bristol Sound'. The Pop Group, the Wild Bunch, Neneh Cherry, Massive Attack, etc. all formed their music – that distinctive, gloomy blend of almost every other genre around at the time – in Bluesies and parties all over St Paul's, protected from the police by the new covenant won by the rioters.

The Tesco Riots

Some like to say that freedom is all about choice. But in the case of the Tesco Riots, there were many who saw freedom as a right *not to choose*. If you need a bottle of milk, say, and you're inside and comfy and can't be bothered, chances are you will go to the nearest possible shop – even if by going to that shop you may be damaging a local business whom you wish to support. The lady in the nice shop with a post office at the top of Stokes Croft has a really, really lovely smile. It's a famous smile. The smile and the human around it are quite literally *infinitely preferable* to an automated checkout machine. Some would argue that the freedom of that community rests on not being able to not choose that smile.

It was in obeisance to such a view that the people of Stokes Croft and environs launched a campaign to oppose the opening of a new Tesco Metro on Cheltenham Road. Of course, local businesses got behind the effort and everyone had a jolly good time of it. Unfortunately for them it wasn't successful, and the Tesco Metro was quickly built by some nanobots or whatever.

It's an interesting one with regards to freedom, because you could make an argument that Tesco should have the freedom to trade there, and the campaign was a direct assault on that freedom. But, of course, seeing it in the context of Tesco being such a dominant economic power, you could look at their aggressive expansion as an assault on the freedom of independent shops in an area of the city that is defined by its independent businesses. It is common to hear in that part of town that nearby Gloucester Road contains the longest string of independent shops in the country. Anyway, I'm not sure whose side you're on, if you're on any – or even if you care at all. So let's get on with the story. The important thing is that the state was on Tesco's side, and they were prepared to put the boys in blue at the front line to prove it. And so it was that yokels armed with pitchforks and torches met a line of police guarding their intended victim. They had come to burn the store to the ground and found themselves in a pitched battle with police.

Or that's how one version of the story goes. Another is very different indeed. To understand this one you are going to have take a trip with me into a very dark underworld, an underworld rich with character and gnarled with story. The squat scene in Bristol has been thriving for a long time. There have been many legendary squats, from the Silver Moon Unlimited crew in a manor house up at Durdham Park, to the Invisible Circus' sojourn at the Audi Garage on Cheltenham Road. The subculture that operates these places is various, confused, confusing, colourful, warped, violent, emotional, romantic, utopian, dystopian, bruised, brave, bold, nefarious, obnoxious, joyous, cliquey, labyrinthine, highly charged, highly sexed, highly politicised, creative, dogmatic, spiritual, dangerous, alarming, unbelievable, unreasonable, difficult to placate, and much else besides. For a storyteller like me to go into a thriving squat to ask a few leading questions is very much what it is like, I imagine, for a soil scientist to thrust her hand into the earth, take a nice handful of the stuff to her nose, and just have a good long sniff. I could really write a book about the scene, but I will limit myself here to just a few pertinent slices of context. Let's take a look at the sizable squatting community in Stokes Croft at the time of the riots. First, there were the homeless who squatted out of convenience. Regarding the riots, they were innocent of anything more serious than a badly timed piss. Then there were the political squatters, who were naturally the ones most drawn to the campaign against Tesco. Then there were assorted musicians and music makers who really didn't know they were squatting, because they really lived in their music. There were the scallywags, who often masqueraded as one of the other types, but who were in truth only in the scene to exploit clownish opportunities as they arose. And finally there were the spiritual squatters, who were split into a bewildering multitude of subcategories, including Pagan, Satanist, Satan's Elect, Buddhist, Anarcho-Buddhist, Wiccan, Mystic-Atheist, Sophtie, Big Sophtie, Sophtie-Philosophical, Filthy, Freaky, Kabalic, Crowley Kabalic, Perverse Crowley Kabalic, Made-Up Ancient Egyptian Stuff, Sex Stuff, Yoga, Yoga-ish, Angry Yoga, Flat Earther, Natural Way, Natural Anger, Native Ways, Santo Daime, Shaman, Relaxed Shaman, Confused Shaman, Mansplainy Shaman, Nihilist, Nihilistic Health Fixation, Strict Nihilistic Health Fixation, Purity Obsession, Eating Disorder, Manichean, Millenarian, Cathar, Great Freedom Teaching, Anarcho-Magical, Kaos Magic, Witch, Black Witch, White Witch, Rainbow Witch, Vague Witch, Witchy Witch, Wishy-Washy, Wasted-Mystical, Plain-Wasted,

K Hole, and various streams of Armageddon-focused 'End Times' sub-subgroups. Across these sundry spiritual factions runs the only distinction that matters in respect to this story: *Light* and *Dark*.

Two practitioners from the 'Dark' side *ate* approximately two people in the decade preceding the Tesco Riots. These ritualistic devourings were apparently consensual or at the very least semi-consensual. A companion of Katie Louche, one of my key informants, was apparently keen to volunteer to be eaten by this pair also, but luckily she talked him out of it. Anyway, this is by the by, for the story of the Tesco riots actually concerns some spiritual squatters of the 'Light' variety. They were residents of the squat known as Telepathic Heights that was pretty much opposite the proposed Tesco store. The Heights had been in the hands of many crews, but at the time of the unfolding of the drama under discussion it had been seeded by the nearby Magpie squat and had become all kinds of spiritual with a heavy inflection toward the Light side of things. Squatters are capable of unifying as a group on occasion, depending on what they face, but often the various factions find themselves in dispute. In Telepathic Heights at the time of the riots, the spiritual faction had long been in struggle with the political faction. The dispute was broadly around whether the response to neoliberal capitalism should be: a) an immediate and mercilessly violent uprising, or b) the creation of utopian communities based around light drug use and positive vibes. Both solutions have much to commend them, and personally I favour a 'best of both worlds' pick-and-mix approach. However, the dispute was there, and, of course, the focus of the debate became what to do now that Tesco was on the eve of opening.

Now, a few scallywags had also set up residence in Telepathic Heights, or technically *on* it, because they lived on the roof in tents. These scallies had taken the side of the politicals, perhaps on a coin toss, or maybe because it seemed the politicals' plan of violent anti-Tesco fightback presented more opportunity for clownish hijinks. They had encouraged the politicals to arm themselves in preparation for the coming world revolution that was inevitably to follow the outrage generated by the opening of the new Tesco Metro on Cheltenham Road. To their delight, the politicals had taken the bait and started to make Molotov cocktails and store them on the roof of the squat. This severely angered the spiritual brigade, who had needed those very bottles for their Kombucha.

After one very nasty argument, which the scallies had created by some very skilled stirring of resentments, one of the Light-side spiritual guys had gone nuclear and snitched to the police about the Molotov cocktails. When the police arrived to raid Telepathic Heights, the squat community banded together and tried to defend the place. It was barricaded and the spirituals, politicals and scallies were all holed up together trying to push back a tide of rozzers. In the general commotion that followed some people decided that then would be a good time to destroy Tesco.

Whatever you believe about how it began (and I urge you not to believe any of what I have written here, for it is certainly utter garbage) the battle raged all that night. There were around 200 officers, decked out in riot gear and riding horses. There were at least as many rioters, brandishing dustbin lid shields and ready with an assortment of improvised projectiles. One of my informants, Rosie Bird, who had only gone to innocently purchase some delicious Jamaican food from Rice N Ting, happened to be present at one of the cavalry charges. Rosie ducked into a doorway, desperate to protect her precious payload of Saltfish, Ackee and dumplings, steamed veg on the side, with extra hot sauce and a patty for tomorrow. She found she was sharing this doorway with a boy who had obviously gone to some effort to dress himself up in the most authentically revolutionary clobber he could get a hold of, and it was clearly making him feel like he was a Banksy stencil. Catching the eye of a copper who was charging toward them on a horse, the bandana-clad youth jiggled two fingers up at him defiantly. The policeman swings with his truncheon, the fella ducks, and poor Rosie Bird cops the full force of the blow, destroying her elbow and crushing her delicious takeaway meal.

It was an impressive ruck. However, although the fires raged, although both rioters and police had their fill of exciting violence, and although the nascent minimart copped it from a few well-aimed bricks and Molotovs, today if you go to Cheltenham Road you'll find a Tesco Express open between 7 a.m. and 7 p.m. daily. Initially a boycott was promised in the strongest terms, but after the store opened Bristol's resolve soon crumbled under a deluge of deals. For instance, I'm told that Comfort Fabric Conditioner is currently half price and that Pilgrim's Choice cheddar cheese has a whopping £2 off, making it virtually half price. Nescafé is also enjoying a generous discount, and I'm not sure if you have a dishwasher or not, but the Finish All-In-One Lemon Dishwasher Tablets Mega Value Pack is reduced to £9.99, meaning each individual tablet only costs £0.12. Furthermore, if you go towards closing then you'll find many perishable goods have really significant reductions as the store tries to clear stock that cannot be sold the next day. The good news is that they now put these reduced goods in one place to give you bargain hunters an easier time of it. Happy shopping!

The Great Insurrection

To those who've learnt anything at all about freedom from these stories then well done. The rest of us have one last chance. I am about to tell you a really remarkable story, and one with a unique place in Bristol's canon of urban legends. Here lies the oldest tale that the people of our fair city are still going on about: The Great Insurrection. Our dear forbears, as you will soon learn, outdid us in the ambition, scale and pure daring of their rebellion.

No one ever gives me a date for The Great Insurrection, and so I shall not give you one. It happened after the Normans but before the Civil War, and that's as specific as anyone gets. I couldn't resist doing some book research on this one, to see what historians say about it, and I strongly suggest that you do the same. As always, the historical story is a lot racier and more exciting than the folk version. True, the thrills these historians go for are rather cheap, but then they are very enjoyable. Please save the guilty pleasure for holiday reading though, for here we must look at what Bristol itself remembers about this remarkable set of events. The details, such as are still knocking around town, are as follows.

A secretive cabal of rich and powerful mercantile interests had gradually been growing in power. Through various prominent merchant and mariner companies, along with the guilds, they were exerting a stranglehold on the city's industries and taking an exorbitant wedge of the hard-working people's revenue. The yeomanry and commoners, along with gentry excluded for one reason or another by the companies, were fed up of the yoke under which they laboured. The problem was that these companies all had the King's Privileges. This was, of course, long before the free market, and to be a company you had to have the support of the Crown. Worst of all, the King had installed a constable in the castle, a really vile and weak-minded chap called Lord Bartholomew de Badlesmere. He was too feckless and happy with his duck eggs and sweetmeats to do anything other than whatever the companies ordered him to do. This meant that the soldiers at the castle were just a de facto private army of mercantile interests. The people of Bristol had very few political options. They suspected, correctly, that a secret society was at the heart of all this, and that very possibly they had inducted the King himself into their club, and thus even he would be duty bound to look at their interests as his own.

Now, there was a very popular mayor and MP of the time, whose name was John Tavener. He was as big as a tree, and just as strong. He had a good heart and genuinely wanted the best for his fellow Bristolians. For a long while he urged people to show restraint, to try and work within the bounds that the constable and the companies set. But one evening, after he had watched the execution of some poor fisherman who had tried, in desperation, to sneak a part of his catch past the official on the harbourside, he sat at his kitchen table and wept. Bristol could be a place bustling with activity, awash with the sounds of a happy, prosperous people. But instead the citizens groaned against the oppression of the companies and the constable in his fortress.

John's wife Sarah came to where he sat, looking long into the fire. She placed her slender hand upon his neck, which was thick as an elephant's leg. His flesh was hot from his worrying. He had grown feverish with confused anger and self-loathing. Sarah's hand was cool as a pebble. She reminded John of his strength, of the people's trust in him. She spoke to him of duties, not to the Crown, but to his fellows. She reminded him that God enters the fray upon the side of the just. Tavener's heart was buoyed as he looked at his wife. If she believed in the cause, then he could believe, too. If he could believe, then Bristol could. They began immediately.

I like imagining the furtive conversations that took place that night. I like imaging the children sent on errands, how they ran through the narrow alleys carrying breathless messages. I wonder what it was like to hear of the insurrection, to hear the word '*Tonight!*' and to have to quickly make up your mind as to whether to join and what to bring. I enjoy wondering where the people chose to meet, and picturing how the nervous chatter of the crowd turned to bravado as the entire town marched over Bristol Bridge. Best of all would have been to see the constable's face as he looked from the tower of the castle out across the wall and saw a sea of faces, lit by torchlight, staring back at him.

The battle raged for days. The King authorised Badlesmere to take over and impose martial law. The town was to be deprived of all liberties and all citizens were to be viewed as enemy combatants. Tavener and the other ringleaders were immediately outlawed. But these were just words, and the people of Bristol had acted. Pitchforks proved themselves mightier than swords. The people drove back Badlesmere's soldiers, along with many company men, into the castle. They then did something shockingly simple and effective. They built a wall around the wall of the castle. No one inside is allowed out. It is not a siege but rather a quarantine of the cancerous element of power. The fortress that was meant to keep Bristol obedient to the Crown has become a prison for the leaders of the old order.

The people vote. John Tavener is elected leader. A republic is declared, free from the Crown and independent of the rest of the country. The King is furious and releases a flurry of edicts. But the Bristol Republic ignores royal edicts. Anyway, all the soldiers are tied up in some pointless foreign war, a vanity project no doubt spearheaded by a sly cosmopolitan thug in the royal court. Even if they were on English soil, who's to say that the men so frequently asked to die for such fancies wouldn't just side with the townsfolk over the Crown?

In the republic, taxes were fair. The poor had relief: no one went hungry in Bristol. Laws were decided by the people for the benefit of all. They even had their own currency. Tavener took a walk across town every morning, over the bridge, past the harbour and up St Michael's Hill. He would turn to take it all in. *Ah, Brizzle!* He wished he could wrap his huge arms around it and give it a hug. It was a place bustling with activity, awash with the sounds of a happy, prosperous people.

Of course, the Bristol Republic doesn't last forever. Some people tell me a year; some say five or ten. It doesn't matter so much, not in terms of what the story means for us today. What matters is that we were free; for a few glorious moments at least, the whole damn town was free.

ABOUT THE AUTHOR

WILF MERTTENS is a poet and storyteller. He tours as a performer, develops and delivers workshops in storytelling and public speaking, and just about scrapes by. He regularly works for the charity Read for Good, telling stories in children's hospitals.

www.wilfmerttens.co.uk